PETER CORRIS was born in Victoria, but is now an enthusiastic resident of Sydney, which has provided the locale for his other Cliff Hardy stories. He was originally a historian, but would now classify himself as a journalist and thriller writer.

Peter Corris

DEAL ME OUT

A Cliff Hardy novel

UNWIN PAPERBACKS
Sydney London Boston

For Di Hawthorne and
  Damien Broderick

First published in Australia
by Unwin Paperbacks 1986

UNWIN® PAPERBACKS
Allen & Unwin Australia Pty Ltd
8 Napier St, North Sydney, NSW 2060, Australia

UNWIN PAPERBACKS
18 Park Lane, Hemel Hempstead,
Herts HP2 4TE, England

National Library of Australia
Cataloguing-in-Publication entry:
Corris, Peter, 1942– .
  Deal me out.

  ISBN 0 86861 978 7 (pbk.).

A823′.3

Typeset in 9.5/11pt Century by
Graphicraft Typesetters Ltd, Hong Kong
Printed by The Dominion Press-Hedges & Bell, Victoria

1

WHEN Terry Reeves of Bargain Renta Car rang me, I thought at first that he was up to his old trick—trying to flog off an exmember of his fleet on me. Over the years he'd offered me Commodores, Peugeots, even an '84 Falcon, but I'd remained true to my Falcon which had been born about a decade earlier.

'Terry,' I said, 'you're wasting your time, I'm going to be buried in that car.'

'You probably will be, Cliff. But this is a business call.'

'You mean you're going to give me money, not take money off me?'

'I mean I want you to earn the money by investigating something. That's what you do, isn't it—investigate?'

'Yeah. Lately I've done more money minding and de-bugging than investigating, but I can still remember how it's done.'

'De-bugging?'

'Yeah, it's all the go. People want you to de-bug every-thing, cars, dunnies, the lot. I did a course in it.'

'What does that mean?'

'Means I talked to a bloke in a pub about it. He puts bugs in and he told me how to take them out. He learned it from another bloke in another pub. What's the job?'

'You've got me edgy, Cliff. Better not talk on the phone.'

'Bullshit. Nine times out of ten the only bugs I find've got legs and feelers. What . . .?'

'Just the same I'd rather do it face to face. Come over to the office. And park that wreck a block away at least. I don't want anyone thinking it's one of mine.'

I let him have the last word, which is always good business practice and I couldn't think of a snappy comeback anyway. I worked with Terry as an insurance investigator after I got out of the army and decided I wasn't cut out for the law. We'd been competitive, had disagreements about fires and things gone missing, but got along well. He went into the car rental business about the same time I set up as a private investigator, about fifteen years ago. He'd probably made a hundred times as much money as me and he'd acquired a nice wife and a couple of attractive kids. I'd lost my not so nice wife who'd gone off to have her attractive kids with someone else. I occasionally rented a car from Terry when a job called for it: we'd stayed in touch.

I drove over to his office in Surry Hills on one of those Sydney spring days that remind you of somewhere else warm with car fumes where you've had a good time, like Rome. Terry runs his show right off one of the parking and servicing stations. It had been a no-frills operation that had lately acquired considerable polish, but it was still not unknown for Terry to do a day behind the desk or in the workshop.

I pulled the Falcon into a prominent place beside one of the highly-glossed, bright orange, fuel-injected vehicles, and told the woman in the orange skirt and white blouse who came over to protest that Terry was expecting me. She eyed the car, which is a bit faded and wrinkled, like me.

'I bet he wasn't expecting you to park that here,' she said.

'You're wrong, he insisted on it.'

She sniffed at that and stepped aside. I walked past a line of cars to the glass-walled outer office. It had a big registration desk, some VDTs, pot plants and posters of places you might drive to with Bargain. A waist-high partition is the only barrier Terry puts between himself and his staff; I considered vaulting it, decided against, and pushed open the half door.

Terry had a telephone in his hand and was scribbling on a pad on his desk. He nodded at me, flipped the receiver up to his ear and caught it with his shoulder like a night club performer playing with the mike, then he waved me into a chair with his free hand. I sat down and looked at him; it was an odd experience, regarding an old friend in a new light, as a client. Clients need special looking at, for rust spots and other defects. Terry was a well-built six footer with blond hair going thin on top. He'd played professional football and been a pro runner in his younger days, and he still had a lot more muscle on him than flab. He was one of the few teetotallers I knew who wasn't a dried-out alcoholic.

Terry had always looked ten years younger than his true age, but now it seemed that a few years had jumped in and wrestled him down. His face was thinner than I remembered it and there were strain lines around his eyes and mouth. He said a few quiet, firm words into the phone and hung up. He gave me a welcoming grin, but the expression flicked off his face quickly as if the muscles couldn't hold it.

'Hello, Cliff. You don't look any more brain-damaged than when I last saw you. Have you been taking it easy?'

'Mmm, could be. I seem to be getting more sleep. How's the family?'

'Okay. Let's get to it. I've lost five cars in the last month.'

'Lost?'

'Lost—gone, vanished.'

'You'd be insured, wouldn't you?'

'Of course. But you know the deal: they'll be getting shirty if I report them all, and the premiums next quarter'll kill me. They already take an arm and a leg.'

'How many claims have you made?'

He ran a finger around inside his shirt collar where there seemed to be more room than a good fit required. He was a neat dresser, Terry, who wore white shirts and plain ties. This shirt was a little grubby at the neck and the tie had been knotted too far down. Terry Reeves looking like a country cousin; that was something new.

'One claim,' he said. 'That puts me in an irregular position. I should have claimed for two more, signalled them at least. But word gets around.' He made a dive-bombing motion with his big, freckled hand. 'People get nervous and business goes down. The margins in this game are tight, believe me.'

Another orange-skirted young woman walked into the office and plonked two polystyrene cups of coffee on the desk. Terry's tired face gave a quick, painful smile.

'Thanks, Dot.' He pushed a cup towards me and rummaged in a drawer of the desk. He pulled out some tin foil wrapped pills, released two and washed them down with a swill of coffee. If it'd been me with that load of worry on I'd have had the bottle out lacing up the coffee, but that wasn't Terry. But then, pills weren't Terry either. I took a sip of the coffee and was surprised that it was good espresso.

'I seem to remember that you wanted my mother's maiden name and references from three clergymen before you let me take out one of your cars.' I drank some more coffee and tried to remember the procedure. 'Driver's licence, plastic ... what else?'

'All that, but it didn't do us any good in these cases, or at least in the couple I checked on—all faked. I don't have the time to follow up on all these and I'm rusty. I wouldn't know how to go about it now probably.'

'It hasn't changed much,' I said, 'footslogging, eyestrain . . . .'

'Eyestrain I know about. Look, Cliff, I'm a desk walloper.' He snorted derisively and opened a drawer. 'I made you up a list. I'm good at making up lists.'

He brought out a manila folder, extracted two sheets of paper and pushed them across to me. The first sheet

4

contained five blocks of type, each recording a name, address, licence number, credit card details and information on the car hired: vehicle make and model, mileage recorded, period of hiring etc. There were three Holdens, a Fiat and a Ford Laser. The second sheet carried photostat copies of one personal and one company cheque and three credit card debit slips.

Terry finished his coffee, crumpled the cup and dropped it into his wastepaper bin. 'I checked on the first two— Majors and Stanford, both Holdens. Phoney as a three dollar note—bodgie addresses, crook licences, no money in the bloody accounts. That's about twenty thousand bucks worth of car gone west.'

I grinned at him. 'West?'

'It's no bloody joke, Cliff. A few more and I'm in real trouble.'

I finished my coffee and took a shot at the bin over the desk. Bullseye. 'What do the cops say?'

'What do they ever say? Yes, sir, very sorry, sir, give us the numbers, sir, and we'll keep an eye out. The last time a cop solved a crime in this town was about the time a doctor cured a patient.'

'Can't be that long.' Terry didn't smile, and it looked like time to drop the levity. He'd never been a boastful man but the self-deprecatory crack about making lists had struck me as a fragility that he probably couldn't afford in this kind of business. In any case, the lurk was a new one on me and interesting in that respect. And it seemed to hold out the prospect of travel; I'd been stuck in Sydney too long. It was time to get business-like.

'A hundred and twenty-five a day and expenses, Terry,' I said. 'I'll waive the retainer because you're a friend.'

'No you won't!' He reached for a fat cheque book and wrote rapidly; I could see the seven hundred and fifty dollars from where I sat. I took the cheque and looked at Terry rather than it. There seemed to be something almost furtive about him, and that was the last word you'd normally apply to Terry Reeves. I gave him one of my hard-guy looks.

'Something else you want to say, mate?'

He sighed. 'Shit, you might as well know. We installed cameras behind the desk a year ago. Didn't want to, but the insurance boys insisted on it. We've got pictures of the clients. Snoopy stuff. We destroy the bloody things when the cars come back.'

I snapped my fingers rudely. 'Gimme.'

The manila folder came out again and Terry shoved it across the desk. The photographs were in colour and blown up to postcard size. The camera looked to have been mounted fairly high behind the desk; the pictures showed the customers full face, but in two instances the lens had caught faces in half profile. They weren't good pictures; the light in the office wasn't conducive to photography and the fixed camera made no allowances for subject size—the tops of the heads of two tallish men were lopped off and of a short man and a small woman there was not much more than head and shoulders. I shuffled the pictures until I had three of each, then I leaned forward to study them more closely.

'You see it?' Terry said.

'Just a minute .... Yeah, I think so.'

'Disguises, pretty good ones. Anyone ever tell you that you look like John Cassavetes, the actor?'

'Yeah, but she had designs on my manly body.'

Terry snorted. 'I'm told this sort of thing is pretty easy to do if you know how.' He pinched in his fleshy nose. 'You can fill in this bit and take in that. A make-up expert could turn you into a Cassavetes look-alike. The hair helps.' He reached over and stabbed at one of the photos. 'Wigs, make-up, contacts, their mothers wouldn't know them.'

I nodded, and took one shot of each person. 'Means there's a well-planned operation here. Expensive too.'

'Good returns,' Terry said. 'You get an as-new car for

the cost of the rental deposit, and I try to keep costs down. You get plates, service book . . . .'

I made a stack of the photos and Terry passed me an envelope. I put the pictures in it and tapped the edge against his desk.

'I know this sounds like a psychiatrist, but have *you* got any ideas?'

'No, none.'

'What about the competition? Anyone you've put under pressure getting back at you?'

He shrugged. 'It's a cut-throat game, but it's still an expanding market. I haven't driven anyone to the wall that I know of. Some of the others might be having the same problem.'

'You haven't checked?'

'No way; that'd be letting on what I've lost. That might give rise to talk. A lot of this is expense account stuff; everyone wants a solid firm to do business with. Nothing shonky.'

I examined the typed list. 'Are they all fleet cars—I mean, all that attractive shade of orange?'

'Ochre.' He looked embarrassed when he said it. 'That's what it's called, ochre. No, that's going out. People don't want to advertise that they've got a hire car. It's on the list. The Holdens are . . . orange. The Laser and the others are different colours. They've got a small logo on them, that's all.'

I grunted. 'They don't have to say where they're going, do they?'

'No, just stipulate a period. They're supposed to say if they're going interstate; affects the insurance. None of this lot did. Probably means they went to Perth.'

'You never know, they could be in Surry Hills. Well, I'll follow you up on the checking and try the photos out on a few people. There's a few other possibilities too.'

'Like what?'

'Don't be so negative, Terry. Like the make-up angle;

7

can't be a hell of a lot of people around who can do that stuff.'

'I'm worried.'

'I said: 'Don't worry' and immediately thought of something to worry him. 'Those cars weren't all signed out by the same person, were they?'

'No. Jesus, Cliff, I trust all these people.'

He did, too, and it was a good reason to work for him. I stood up and the phone range. He said 'Yes' into it, and then groaned. 'Which one?' The voice on the line sounded agitated. I sat down again. Terry listened and aged in front of my eyes. 'Okay, okay, calm down. I'm doing something about it right now. Just send in the paperwork as soon as you can, and the pictures. Take your time.'

He put the receiver down gently. He was looking straight through me, and I swivelled my head to look at the wall behind me. There was a big poster of Ayers Rock, looking red and mysterious. I wanted to say that the cars wouldn't be parked behind the rock but I didn't. Terry was undergoing some sort of crisis.

'Another one, fuck it! I'm getting angry.'

'Good. What kind of car?'

'Bloody Audi, only one I've got. There's a special booking for it, too, Shit, that'll cost me money.'

We sat without talking. I studied the typed list and Terry shuffled some papers. After a few minutes the orange skirt swished in. The woman put papers and photographs on the desk, clicked her tongue sympathetically and went out. Terry spread the exhibits.

'Bruce Worthington', he said. 'Company Director, Mastercard, New South Wales licence, blah, blah, usual thing. Out for five days and three days late. See the name? Worthington. What were those others? Majors was one, Sergeant, and the woman was Faith somebody. Jesus!'

'Let's have a look at him.'

I spread the photographs, which were only passport size, peered at them and tried to keep my jaw attached.

The face was lean with deep grooves running down beside the nose to the mouth. The hair was short, not long and wild, and the bushranger beard had been trimmed to a fine line along the jaw ... but it was still the face of Bill Mountain, a fairly close enemy of mine over the past ten years.

2

Terry undid his loose collar and slipped his tie down; he rumpled his thin hair and looked more like a football player than a businessman, but a player in a losing team. I scribbled the details from 'Worthington's' registration form on the back of the typed sheet, selected two of the clearest photographs and slipped them into the envelope. I looked through the other set of photos again and pulled out another two. Terry looked through me as if a graph of his business had suddenly appeared over the Ayers Rock poster.

'Going to be hard to cover that Audi,' he muttered. 'Wonder if he'd settle for a Merc?'

'Probably.' I stood up and passed the photos of the defaulters back across the desk; they had a blank look as if they knew they were only wearing their faces for a day.

'What're you going to do, Cliff?'

I tapped 'Worthington' on the nose. 'Start with the freshest. I'll be in touch, mate. Try not to worry. You can probably take a lot of it off your tax.' I grinned at him. 'You can take me off your tax, too.'

'Yeah.' He summoned up a quick smile. 'When you give me a receipt.'

I let him give me my exit line, and went back into the outer office. His phone rang as I went, and I hoped it wasn't another bolter. A fat man was checking out a car at the desk; I couldn't see the camera, but I could imagine the pictures—very unflattering angle for chins, especially when you've got three of them.

I removed my eyesore from the parking bay, and tried to assemble the randon information I had on Bill

Mountain as I drove to my office at the Cross. Mountain was a writer, of short stories mostly, with a couple of novels. As he told it, the fees he'd got for the stories hadn't paid for the paper and typewriter ribbons; the novels had been raved about in *Meanjin* and remaindered within months. His agent had got even more desperate than Bill and wangled him a crash course in film writing. Mountain took to it like a sailor to sex, and he landed a job writing TV soap operas.

He'd told me this as he worked his way through a bottle of Suntory whisky, his chosen drink. Those grooves in his face seemed to get deeper with every sip, and the rutted lines around his eyes criss-crossd like ski tracks.

'It's a treadmill, Hardy, a bloody treadmill.'

'Is that the kind of dialogue you have to write?' I'd asked. He threw a punch then which I ducked and he fell over. After that it was all apologies and more drinks until the next time. I didn't like Mountain, but we had mutual acquaintances, and I seemed always to be running into him here and there, especially a few years ago when my drinking was nearly in his league. Since then I'd moderated it a bit, and our paths crossed less often, but I heard about him. I heard how he called me an ASIO man, a 'disinformation agent' and other unflattering things. I heard how he hit women in public, and drank all the money he hated earning so fast that he had to go on earning it.

The trouble was that he could be interesting on the subject of writing, and I had a lot of time for some people who seemed to like him. The last time we'd met had been a few months back, in a pub as usual. He'd been sitting with my reporter friend, Harry Tickener, slurping down the Suntory and twitching hairs from his woolly beard into the corner of his mouth, catching them in his teeth and plucking them out with a twitch of his head. It was an unpleasant thing to watch.

'The guys who make up the story lines are even worse

11

than the poor hacks like me who fill them in,' Mountain had said. A hair popped out leaving an angry spot behind. 'Bigger drunks than me, most of 'em. They get paid more so they can afford it. Some go this route,' he'd lifted his glass, 'booze and gambling; some go the other way—religion. I know one outline man who gives it all away to some nutty church.'

Mountain had started to scowl when he could see that I intended to get at least a couple of words in with Harry. Harry played the conciliator.

'How would you handle a straight thousand a week, Cliff?'

'I'd invest it in Bill's next novel. I'd stake him for six months while he wrote it.'

Mountain was hard to gauge, it depended partly on the Suntory level. Right then I'd half expected him to throw the bottle but he tipped it over his glass instead.

'Might as well put it on a bloody horse,' he growled. 'Least you'd get a show. I can't write a novel, haven't had an experience in eight years.'

That was one way to handle Mountain, to plunge him into self-pity and steer him away from aggression. Then, of course, you didn't get his funny stories about the TV industry, his malicious gossip and his very good singing voice—the things people liked him for. With me, it was usually a choice between the self-pity and skinned knuckles and I took the former every time.

I parked the car behind Primo Tomasetti's tattoo parlour and tried to remember how that meeting with Mountain had ended or what had been said. I couldn't, not without effort. It occurred to me that I could probably recall a lot more of Bill Mountain's conversation if I tried, but I didn't think it had ever included anything to suggest he'd take up car theft.

The needle was buzzing in Primo's place and my

respect for art prompted me to sneak past and go up the stairs to my office without interrupting him. But he heard me and switched off.

'Cliff.'

I poked my head around the corner; the young client looked alarmed and pointed at his shoulder. 'She's only got one eye,' he yelped.

'Momento,' Primo said. 'Cliff, I got an idea. I'll do you your Keycard number anywhere you like for fifty cents.' Primo has been trying to tattoo me for years.

'I haven't got a Keycard,' I said.

'No class.' He switched on the needle. I went up one flight and along the passage to my office which also has no class, unless it's fourth class. The city is over-supplied with office space although they're building more all the time. Some of the over-supply is right here in my building as well as much of the turnover. In the years I've been here a lot of people have moved out but never because their expanding business needed room to grow. I noticed that we'd been joined by an ESP consultant, whatever that was. It was all right with me; it sounded like a nice quiet pursuit.

Two days' absence from the office had generated some junk mail and the registration renewal papers for the Falcon. I wrote out the cheque thinking that there should be a prize for keeping old cars on the road or at least a sliding scale of registration fees. Instead I had a registration inspection to pass. I stuck a thirty-three cent stamp on the envelope and wondered if I'd live to see the dollar stamp, standard mail. Probably.

Then I spread the photos out on the desk with the ones of Mountain in the middle. I'd intended to commune with them, searching for a pattern, but I found myself thinking exclusively of Mountain again. The haircut and beard trim made him look less bulky but he was one of those men whom drinking fined down rather than made fat. If he was actually thinner it could be due to the Suntory. He looked harder though; the grooves were the size of my little finger and the line of beard hair followed the sharp ridge of his jawbone.

Action. I rang the TV production company he worked for and asked for him. A syrupy-voiced woman told me that Mr Mountain was on a month's leave which still had two weeks to run. I'll say this for Mountain, he doesn't go in for this pretentious silent number business. He was listed as 'Mountain, Bill' in Bondi Junction. I dialled the number and it rang and rang until I fancied I could see the emptiness of the room all around the instrument.

A few more calls brought the expected results: 'Bruce Worthington's credentials were worthless. He'd given 'film and TV producer' as his occupation and the Polyglot Film Company as his place of business. Like all the phone numbers on the defaulters' list this one had been circled and ticked, indicating that it had been checked. But it's not too hard to arrange for someone to answer a phone and say what the caller wants to hear. Takes organisation though.

I was getting sick of looking at these uninspired photographs already; they reminded me of the videos of bank robberies where the sets look phoney and the actors can't act ... but they caught crooks. Mountain looked to be sober in the pictures, in control of himself. He didn't look relaxed, but then he never did and wasn't. He also didn't look as if someone had a gun trained on him from across the street or had his old mum tied up to the kitchen table.

I had another job in the offing just then, a piece of body-guarding nonsense for a man who thought he might be mentioned soon in a crime report. He probably wouldn't be. I off-loaded the late nights and sore feet on a man who was glad of the work. Terry Reeves' missing cars and Bill Mountain's new life of crime held a lot more interest.

I drove home to Glebe in the late afternoon and had to

14

stop for groceries because I was living alone again. My lodger for the past three years—Hilde Stoner—had moved in with Frank Parker who held the rank of Detective Sergeant in the New South Wales police. She was pregnant and they were happy. Frank's career was progressing again. I occasionally went over to Harbord where they lived and Frank beat me on the tennis court. He couldn't beat Hilde though.

Helen Broadway and I had an arrangement. She spent half a year in the country with her husband and child and half a year in the city with me. I thought it was mighty decent of Michael Broadway to oblige in this way, but Helen said he hardly noticed the difference between her periods of residence and absence. The deal suited everybody except perhaps the kid who didn't get a say.

Helen had left two weeks before to begin her wife-in-residence segment. We'd had an exhaustive and exhausting sexual session and in the morning she was gone. So now I had an empty house that still bore traces of a woman's recent presence. I was enjoying the solitude and would for about a week more; but already I was regretting that Helen wouldn't be there for the summer.

I threw together something to eat and allowed myself two glasses of wine. When it got dark I put on jeans, sneakers and a black T shirt, collected a leather pouch of pick locks and keys and went off to do a little discreet burglary.

Bill Mountain lived in a part of the Eastern Suburbs that was called Bondi Junction by some and Centennial Park by others. In fact the park was right opposite the row of small houses. I'd been there to a party a couple of years back and recalled the laneway behind the house and the brick wall with some sort of creeper over it. From recollection it was the sort of wall a man in reasonable health could get over without a ladder. We burglars

15

weren't carrying ladders that year.

I drove carefully around the district in the despised Falcon to get the feel of the place. I parked a couple of blocks away on the principle that quick getaways were easier on foot than by car, especially with the open acres just across the way. As I walked through the streets I pondered on how much easier burglary was when the burglar had had social entry to the house beforehand. Nothing new; Raffles had proved that.

The traffic was light, but it was a fine night and there were a few people in the streets so I had to lurk at the entrance to the laneway for a bit before I could slink down it to tackle the wall. Mountain's place was three from the end. I slunk quickly, took a quick look left and right and swung up onto the wall. The creeper helped. The backyard was small and mostly bricked over; some light from the house next door fell on the bricks and helped me to miss the potplants and little herb garden as I came down.

I stood still by the back of the house listening for sounds of humans or other animals. It was quiet. The bush with leaves like a tomato plant growing by the back door surprised me; most people as alcohol-pickled as Mountain don't get anything out of the stuff.

I rattled the back door and let the sound soak into the silence inside. Still nothing. I ran a thin torch beam around the edges of the doors and windows looking for wires and electric cells, but Mountain had opted for a simpler security. The lock was tricky, new and dead-locked, but the picks were new and tricky too. The lock yielded after a while; the door had a sliding bolt in place but there's a tool for that too. All in all, it was one of my quieter and smoother entries.

It's a mistake to creep around in strange houses trying to avoid the furniture and glassware by torch light. You bump into things, it looks suspicious from the outside and you can't really see anything useful anyway. Put on a few lights and the telly, bung on a kettle and no-one looks or listens twice.

I did all that, and prowled through the house. The small sitting room in front had a few ornaments and pictures and a shotgun hanging over the fireplace. Otherwise the house was dominated by books, manuscripts, magazines and newspapers. They overflowed in all rooms including the bathroom and toilet. There was enough paper in the house to re-constitute a small forest. I stood at a bookcase and flicked through magazines, galley proofs and scrapbooks stacked in with expensive hardback novels. I had no idea what I was looking for—just impressions—but nothing was revealed unto me.

Mountain's workroom was a study in chaos: there was a big desk with an electric typewriter sitting on it, but paper had flowed over the machine like lava over a hill. The surface was covered by words ranging from a volume of the Encyclopaedia Britannica to a tiny three line death notice clipped from a newspaper. The desk drawers were full of notepaper, lined and unlined pads, pens, filing cards, paper clips and bits of string. I remembered looking into the room some time back at the party Mountain had got up on the spot at the pub the way he liked to do. The room looked the same now as then.

In the bedroom the bed was a tangle of sheets and blankets and the clothes in the wardrobe looked disorganised but intact. There was food and wine in the fridge and half a case of Suntory whisky in a kitchen cupboard.

Following the policy of acting natural, I went into the bathroom for a piss. There were two toothbrushes and the usual accessories. Washing my hands, I found the first independent confirmation that Mountain was 'Worthington'. In the hand basin, only partly washed away, was a scattering of beard clippings. There were more on the floor. I didn't sweep them up and put them in an envelope but the find jogged memories of Mountain moving around in his house, pouring drinks and . . . hanging his car keys on a nail in the kitchen.

I went through to the back, found the keys and put them on the table. They rattled, and a clinking sound came from the front of the house like an answer. I went cautiously down the passage towards the sitting room. There was a chair standing in front of the fireplace and the shotgun was missing from above it. I gaped at the space and started to turn towards the door. Before I completed the turn I heard the hammers click back and a voice cut in through the sound: 'Stand right there and don't move or I'll shoot you.'

3

WHEN someone holding a gun says 'Don't move', what they really mean is don't pull out a bigger gun or reach for an axe. I continued my turn, but slowly. When I stopped I was facing the shotgun. It was held by a young woman who couldn't have been much taller than the gun was long; but she held its weight steadily enough. She wore a white overall on top of a dark turtle neck skivvy; her high-heeled boots might have lifted her over five feet, just. The only other remarkable thing about her, apart from the shotgun, was that she was Chinese.

'How did you get in?' I said stupidly.

She shifted the gun a little and I thought I might be able to wait her out. Maybe eventually she'd have to put the gun down from sheer fatigue. But she wasn't tired yet. She shook back some of the short, black hair that hung in a fringe over her eyebrows. She had an oval face with a broad nose and wide mouth; those features went admirably with her slanted eyes. I'd never seen a better-looking shotgun holder.

'I came through the bloody door. What about you?'

'Through the back window.'

Our voices and accents were alike; she couldn't have been born any further east than Bondi. I suppose we could have been excused our tones: mine was nervous and hers was angry.

'What for? There's nothing much to steal here.'

'That'd take a bit of explaining,' I said. 'Could you put the gun down?'

She shook her head; the fringe danced.

'D'you know where Bill Mountain is?' I didn't know

19

what to do with my hands so I clasped them in front of me like a clergyman.

'You know Bill?' She sounded more concerned than angry now, and her attention slipped away from the gun a little.

'I've had the odd drink with him. I've been here to a party once. Put the shotgun down. I'll explain.'

Like any sane person, she was looking for an excuse to put the gun back on the wall, but she hadn't found it yet. Her pure Sydney accent got the harsh edge to it we develop when things don't go our own way.

'What's your name?'

'Cliff Hardy.'

'Never heard of you.'

'Why should you? I'm a private investigator. I can show you the ID. I'm looking for Bill.'

'Oh shit! That's all I need!' She moved the hand on the stock up to join the other one on the barrel; then she leaned the gun against the wall like a broom. I breathed out fully for the first time in minutes and unclasped my hands. She got a packet of cigarettes and matches out of the back pocket of her overall and lit up in a smooth, unhurried movement. She sat down on the arm of the couch and put the spent match back in the box. From that point, about three feet off the floor, she blew smoke up at me; she squinted against the smoke and her eyes disappeared altogether—very disconcerting.

'You're after the alimony then?' she said.

'I didn't know he was married.'

'Twice.'

'I'm not interested in any alimony. It's a bit hard to explain. Could I sit down?'

She waved the hand holding the cigarette and I plonked myself down in one of Mountain's easy chairs. My legs felt stiff and old. The shotgun leaned against the wall equidistant from us, but she seemed to have lost interest in it. She drew deeply on the cigarette.

'Hard to explain, you said. Probably bullshit.'

I tried to look like a non-bullshitter. 'No, but it's not exactly a public matter. Could I ask who you are?'

'Erica Fong. I'm Bill's girlfriend or whatever you call it. Or I was—not sure now. Let's see this ID you mentioned.'

I took out the wallet that contains the investigator's ticket, and leaned forward to pass it over to her. I brought the hand back, took hold of the shotgun, and moved it along the wall closer to me. She appeared not to notice. She looked at the licence, shrugged and handed it back.

'I just might have heard him mention you. Is that likely?'

'Depends on what you were talking about and how much he'd had to drink.'

'What does he ever talk about? How he hates the crap he writes and ....'

'And what?'

'Why do you want him, Mr Hardy?'

That was the crunch. Here we were in Bill Mountain's front room, me in my burglar gear and her in what I now realised was a ski suit and getting along so well and I had to tell her that I was after her bloke for stealing a car. Tricky. She threw her cigarette butt into the fireplace and leaned back watchfully.

'It's to do with a car,' I said.

'A car! No-one has adventures in cars anymore—not since Kerouac.'

Adventures, I thought, *who said anything about adventures*?

'Have you read Kerouac?' she said.

'*On the Road*, that's all. Long time ago.'

'I haven't. I haven't read anything. I just picked that up from Bill. I've picked up a lot of stuff like that. If you say Harold Pinter I can name a couple of plays, but I haven't seen them.' She reached back for her cigarettes and matches, lit the cigarette and tossed the match into the fireplace. It landed neatly beside the butt. She drew in the smoke and her tough voice started to waver.

'Bill said he'd take me to all the plays.' She sniffed. 'He said I could read all the books too, but he could never find the right ones in all the mess.' She was crying now, quietly with her cigarette burning down between her fingers and her slim shoulders shaking.

I let her cry, and occupied myself by breaking open the shotgun, removing the shells and replacing the weapon on the mantelpiece. Erica Fong got control of herself, got the cigarette back up to her mouth and took a drag. Her tear-stained face was in profile, firm-chinned and strong. She didn't wipe her face and I got the feeling that she hadn't cried very often.

'I haven't seen Bill for three days,' she said. 'This is the fourth. I was used to seeing him every day and most nights. I'm very worried about him.'

'How long have you known him, Erica?'

''bout a year. I know he's a drunk and everything, but he's a lovely man really. We were going to go to China together. He was going to show me things.' She sniffed and drew on the cigarette. 'He's been there before and he speaks Cantonese. Isn't it funny? I don't speak a word of Chinese.'

I gave her one of my semi-professional smiles; I was feeling very confused and in need of something to stimulate thought. When you burgle a place you expect creaking boards and cats, not non-Cantonese-speaking Chinese girls with shotguns.

'Can we make a cup of tea or something, a drink? We've got a pretty tricky situation here.'

Socially speaking, it should have been more awkward than it was—the Occidental burglar and the Oriental girlfriend, but a strange sort of harmony grew between us in the kitchen as she made instant coffee, using the spoons and utensils with familiarity.

I fiddled with Mountain's car keys at the table while the water was boiling. She smoked non-stop, practically lighting one cigarette from another, and the smoke hung heavily with the steam in the still, small kitchen. One part at least of her story checked out: the milk in Mountain's fridge was a week old and had gone off. When the coffee was ready she sat down opposite me and put three heaped spoonsful of sugar into hers and stirred vigorously. Her lean figure suggested that this was something new. She sipped and puffed.

'Are you running on coffee and cigarettes, like in the movies?'

'Yes.'

'Hasn't Mountain ever taken off somewhere for a few days before? He's not Mr Steadfast as I recall him.'

'No. He hasn't.' Puff. Sip.

'You were going to say something else back there a bit.' I tried to recall the conversation. 'Something about other things on his mind apart from his crappy work.'

She looked angry again. 'You don't like him, do you?'

'I was just trying to get the words right.'

'But you don't like him?'

I shrugged and drank some more coffee. It wasn't a good brand and they always taste worse black. 'It's not relevant. It's not a personal matter.'

'What sort of matter is it then? All I know is that it's about a car.'

'I can't tell you. I've got a client and his business is confidential. It's serious, the part involving Mountain I mean, but it's not life and death.'

'You're going to have to tell me more than that.'

'How can I? All I know about you is that you can handle a shotgun and you've made coffee here before.'

She stubbed out her cigarette in the saucer and almost upset the cup. 'You've got a bloody nerve! All I know about you is that you sneak around in other people's houses.'

I grinned at her. 'If Mountain was here d'you reckon he'd think this was good dialogue?'

She smiled, and it was as if her face had been waiting days to do it. It was a good smile. 'He might. I don't know.

23

Did you ever see him do a send-up of the stuff he writes?'

'Yes. Hilarious. What did he call the show — Tumourville?'

'That was one name, there were lots of others. Oh God, I might as well finish the thought I had before. He seemed to be talking a lot more about wanting to write a novel and needing some more experience to do it.'

'I've heard him talk like that.'

'Mm, well, it seemed to be getting more and more important to him. He took leave from the TV job a while back to work on the novel. I told him he'd had all the experience he needed—two wives, kids, God knows how many women.'

I murmured, 'Fights,' and she glanced sharply at me.

'I suppose so. He wouldn't listen. On and on about life and experience. First he drops out of sight and now you turn up. I was worried before, but I'm really worried now.'

'Why? He's a grown man.'

'It's this word *experience*. D'you know what kind of stories he wrote? What that novel of his was about?'

I shook my head.

'Weird stuff. Crime. Horror.'

'I thought it got a good review in *Meanjin*?'

'Oh, it had "art" in it as well, but it was *about* what I say.'

'And it still didn't sell?'

She shook her head. 'Bill wouldn't let me read it. He didn't keep a copy himself.'

'Maybe it needed more crime and horror.'

I looked down at her and wondered how old she was. Under thirty, I judged but it was hard to tell. I realised that one of the interesting things about her was that I had no idea what she was going to say next. This time she looked away from me, spoke slowly and suddenly made me wonder how old *I* was.

'That's not a very bright thing to say,' she said.

After that there didn't seem to be much point in being coy about my enquiry. I told her about the hire car racket and the photograph of Mountain signing out the Audi. She smoked, listened and drank her cold coffee. She didn't know that Mountain had cut his beard. I showed her the clippings in the bathroom.

I stood outside the bathroom and watched her look at herself in the mirror and swish at her fringe. She couldn't see much more than that of her head in the mirror.

'You're sure?'

'Unless he's got a twin brother who's knocked himself about in the same way.'

She shook her head. 'The silly bastard.'

'That's right, he's going the right way to get experience. He'll get some courtroom experience and be able to write some good, graphic stuff about life in Long Bay.'

She pushed past me and got back to the kitchen and her cigarettes. 'You've got no idea where he'd take the car?' she said gloomily. 'He didn't have to say?'

'No. Did he talk to you about this book? I mean, did he give you any idea of what it was about? Where it's . . . set? Would he have made a plan?'

She jumped up from the table. 'He might have. He made plans for some things.' I followed her out of the kichen into the workroom. She leafed through and shuffled the papers that were on the desk, those that were lying on top of a drawer that had been pulled out like a tray and all the ones that had fallen on the floor. After a while she looked up at me through the fringe.

'All TV stuff.'

I nodded and poked around the room. The bookcases lining the walls were crammed full, with the spaces above the upright books occupied by others lying flat. The desk was set to face a wall rather than a window and books stood upright with their spines facing outward along the whole of its length. I glanced idly along the row, noting a few familiar titles, a thesaurus, dictionaries, a dictionary of quotations, histories and biographies. My eye stopped at a clutch of six paperbacks. Unlike the other books on the desk which were thumbed and battered, these were brand new. I pulled them out.

'What does he read mostly—fiction?'

She was sitting on a swivel chair that was mounted on runners. She stretched out her leg and pushed off from the desk so that the chair ran back a few feet. The white ski overall was the perfect garment for her; she looked small and tough and smart and ready to be a lot of fun if the right opportunity presented. She'd run out of cigarettes so she stuck her hands inside the bib of the overall, presumably to keep from chewing the nails or doing something worse.

'Fiction? No, not that much. Sometimes, but more biographies, plays . . . .'

I held out the paperbacks and let her read the authors' names and the titles. She shook her head. 'What?'

'Mysteries,' I said, 'detectives. Look—Michael Lewin, Sjowall and Wahloo, Maigret, for Chrissake.'

'So what?'

'It's bad enough if he decides to get some first hand experience of crime but this stuff makes it look as if he's interested in *solving* the bloody crimes. Justice and all that.'

I put the books down on the desk; their shiny newness was marred by rough turning down of the corners of a couple of pages at a time. Each book had three or four of these corner folds which suggested that Mountain had consumed the books in a couple of gulps. Twenty-five dollars' worth of dangerous dreams.

'Undercover?' Erica Fong said.

'He couldn't be that dumb.'

She nodded her head vigorously and withdrew her hands from the bib. Her fists were clenched tight. 'He could be. Yes he could! God, I need a cigarette.'

4

T HE idea that Mountain might have gone out playing
Lone Ranger was the first bright thought I'd had since
meeting Erica Fong, and it didn't do either of us any good.
I'd told her enough about the car racket, the false papers
and disguises and so on, to give her the tip that it was an
organised business. You don't have to live very long in
Sydney to become aware that organised criminality is
something to stay away from. The Harbour is too conve-
niently close.

Erica rooted through Mountain's papers again and
found a half packet of his Gitanes. While she was
coughing her way into the first cigarette and I was wishing
there was something else to drink in the place besides
black instant and Suntory whisky, I had my second bright
idea. Mountain must have got on to the strength of the
car-stealing team through someone else, perhaps one of
the people in my picture gallery. I described a couple of
the faces to Erica from memory, but I didn't do it very
well.

'I'd have to see them,' she said, 'and even then I don't
know. He knows a lot of people I don't. He met a lot in
pubs, people like you.'

I took that as a sign that she'd had enough of my
company for the night.

'I've got the pictures in my office. Would you come in
tomorrow morning and take a look?'

'Sure.'

We left it there. She let me out through the front door
and I handed her the shotgun shells and one of my cards
as I left.

She rolled up to the office at around ten the next morning. She was wearing designer jeans and a scoop-neck black knitted top that had cost money. So had the bag she dropped carelessly on the floor as she sat in my client chair. Out came the cigarettes and her impassive look gave way to one of impatience.

I hadn't liked the job much at first and it wasn't getting any better. I wasn't in the mood for impatient young women. I took the envelope out of my desk slowly, tapped it on the scarred surface and looked owlishly over at her.

'Do you mind telling me what you do for a living, Miss Fong?'

She sighed and puffed irritably. Then she smiled. 'At least you got the name right. On second meeting people usually call me Wong.'

'Can't understand it.'

'I don't do anything much. My Dad's got an import business, Hong Kong and China. I go on the odd trip for him and do a bit of decorating in the shops.'

I nodded and slid the photos out onto the desk. She butted her cigarette and pulled her chair up close.

'I'd like to see Bill first, please.'

I spread the pictures out with Mountain in the middle and moved away to give her a bit more of the dim light my dirty windows afford.

I watched her face as she picked up the photo of Mountain. She studied it closely and nodded. She gave a tight smile, brushed back her fringe and tapped the picture with the fingers of her right hand. Her fingernails were cut short and unpainted and her touch was light. I felt a twinge of envy for Bill Mountain.

'He looks good with the beard cut, doesn't he?'

'Yeah. Take a look at the others.'

She put Mountain's picture down and turned her attention to the others.

'Take your time.'

She lit a cigarette and I lifted the window a discreet

28

inch. She held up the picture of Henry Majors.

'I said to take your time.'

Her puff of smoke drifted across the surface of the photograph. 'I don't need to take my time. I know this guy and Bill knows him too. He didn't always have the moustache but I couldn't mistake those eyes.'

Majors' eyes were small and close-set, giving him a slightly lizardy look. His moustache was unconvincing to a sceptical eye, but probably no more than real moustaches. Erica had selected a photo in which Majors was caught looking up from the registration form on which he had been writing. A pair of tinted spectacles was sitting on the desk beside his writing hand. In the other photograph he had the glasses firmly in place and the lizardy look was gone.

'What's his name?'

'I'm trying to think.' For that she seemed to need a new cigarette, and since her Dad owned an import business she could afford to butt out one scarcely smoked and light a new one. She blew smoke at my water-stained wall.

'You don't know any of the others? They're . . . .'

'Shh!'

When half of the cigarette was gone she snapped her fingers. 'Got it. Mal!'

'Mal? Mal who?'

'I don't know; but Bill brought him home from the pub one night. I didn't like him, but he and Bill seemed to hit it off. I don't know what time Bill came to bed, but it was late and he was very drunk.'

'That's the only time you saw him?'

'Yes. But I know that Bill saw him again at least once—for a drink, of course.'

'When was this?'

''bout a month ago, bit less maybe.'

'Well, that makes him look like the contact, but, God, it's not much to go on. Mal—that all?'

'Yes.'

'Okay—big question, what pub?'

She stubbed out the cigarette and looked seriously at me. Her creamy skin was unlined except for a small frown mark between her eyes which was visible through a gap in the fringe. That mark deepened now.

'I can't remember the name, but I can take you there.'

I shook my head. 'Come on, Erica, this is my line of work. You know the name of the place.'

The frown line deepened further. 'I clean forget,' she said.

I laughed. 'Lucky you're not a client; who'd employ a detective that easily caught?'

'I might.'

I shook my head. 'Conflict of interest. You've got me, Erica. You can come along but you'll have to stay in the car.'

'Why's that?'

'If Mal sees you and he's been up to some tricks with Mountain he could get nasty or he could run.' I sat down behind the desk again. Like all the best-looking women, she was impressively stylish in the simple clothes: 'You sort of stand out in a crowd.'

'I'll wear shades and a hat, five inch heels. I'm going too. I'm afraid I hold the whip, Mr Hardy. I'm inviting you along, not asking permission to go.'

I groaned. 'How old are you?'

'Twenty-eight. Why?'

'How'd you get to be so tough?'

She smiled. 'A four foot eleven Chinese girl with four big brothers is tough or she's a door mat. I'm just like everyone else—I like getting my own way. But I'm used to pushing for it.'

'Okay, I'm pushed. Get ready to be bored.'

'How d'you mean?'

'You expect to roll up to the pub about nine tonight and spot him drinking scotch on his own in the saloon bar, don't you? Then we take him aside for a little chat and he tells us all he knows about Bill. That it?'

She didn't say anything but I guessed I'd described her fantasy about right.

'It won't be like that, I can tell you. He won't be there tonight and probably not for several nights, if he shows up at all. He won't want to talk to us and even if he does he won't know much. He'll lie to us. That's the way these things work.'

She pursed her lips and looked determined. 'I was bored for years and years before I met Bill, and I haven't been bored since. I can take a bit of boredom now to get him back. Where will I meet you?'

'How about nine o'clock at the pub?'

She grinned. 'No way—I'm taking you, remember?'

'I feel sorry for your brothers.'

She snorted, picked up her bag and went to the door. She leaned on the handle and looked back enquiringly. I was reluctant to see her go.

'What about having some Chinese food together before we go?'

'Is that supposed to be a joke?'

'No.'

'All right. How about eight at Li's in Randwick.'

'Is that near the pub?'

'Give up, Hardy. See you at Li's.'

She went out and I heard her heels clicking all the way down the quiet, no-business-as-usual corridor.

Li's was too dark to be memorable. I felt my way through the bamboo curtains and the gloom to where Erica sat in a pool of candlelight and cigarette smoke. She'd already ordered; we ate the things that came and we talked— mostly about Mountain, although a little about her. She did every thing decisively: smoked, ate and drank her tea that way, and I began to feel that she was a good ally in the search for Mountain. The only trouble was that she could be a formidable enemy when and if we found him.

One of the nice touches at Li's was that they turned on a small, concealed table light when they presented the bill. Erica insisted on paying half, and we went out into the Randwick night more or less evens, with her information giving her a slight edge.

The pub was in Kensington and had been adopted by the university students, which meant that the management had gone for maximum drinking space and minimum comfort. It had a large, outdoor terrace crammed with chairs, benches and tables in various stages of decay. The two main bars seemed to have been designed to promote deafness; the noise of the juke boxes, TV sets and pinball machines blended in with the raucous blast of Friday night student revelry. Erica had put on shades and high heels as she'd promised, and she looked exotic and mysterious as she peered through the glasses into the loudest bar.

I shook my head. 'Be like drinking in a room with a taxiing 707. Let's go out on the terrace.'

I got a white wine for myself and a gin and tonic for Erica, and we sat on the terrace which was filling up with kids who either didn't like noise or were taking a break from it. There were just enough over-twenty-fives around for us not to look conspicuous.

'Maybe it's not a good night,' I said. 'End of week fun night.'

'It was a Friday that Bill met him. He liked to get into all this on Friday; said it made him feel young.'

'Christ, I can't even remember what young felt like. He's not going to be here, love. You know that.'

'What's this, Hardy's first law of surveillance?'

'Something like that.' I drank a big gulp of wine and waited for it to make me feel young.

'I'm going to take a look around.'

She knocked off her gin and tonic and wandered down through the sprawling bodies, all wearing jeans, all talking and laughing, all young. Blasts of music came from the bar and I held myself tense for a while until I realised what was wrong and relaxed: this wasn't the sort of pub I was used to and I'd been waiting for the sound of breaking glass.

'He's here!' Her voice was a hiss with tobacco and gin.

'Are you sure?'

'See for yourself, he's in the ... what d'they call it? The Scotch Thistle Room or something.'

She meant the slightly lower decibel bar, which had apparently aspired to a Caledonian decor before the student take-over. It had a tartan carpet much eroded by beer and cigarette ash, and framed, glass-covered pictures of Highland scenes, which were mostly obliterated by graffiti scrawled over the glass.

Erica pointed with her chin at the bar and sat down on a spare chair near the door, while I went over for a professional look. Trade was brisk along the length of the bar with the patrons two deep in some places. 'Mal' or 'Majors', call him Mal, got served with two drinks and took them across to a table near the middle of the room where another man and a woman were sitting. He wasn't wearing his sunglasses tonight and his hair looked a few shades lighter than in the photo, but the reptilian eyes were unmistakable.

The woman at Mal's table was about his age, mid-thirties. She was getting fat and trying to hide the fact in clothes too young for her. She didn't worry me; I thought I could handle her.

The man was another story. He kept his eye on Mal as he delivered the drinks, and he didn't seem too interested in his. The arms draped back over his chair would have been too well-developed to hold comfortably close to his torso.

I used the bar toilet and came back to Erica's chair, which she'd turned slightly away from Mal's field of vision.

'No drink?' she said.

'No. We've got a problem.'

'No problem. That's him. We just bowl up and lay it on him.'

'We don't. Did you notice the guy with him?'

She shook her head.

'Not a trained observer, see. He's what we've learned from the television to call a minder.'

'Are you scared of him?'

'I don't know enough about him to know whether to be scared. He's big enough for the work, and he looks like he wouldn't trip over the furniture when he moved. But that's not the real worry. If Mal's got a minder, it means he expects trouble. He doesn't know we're onto him so the trouble must be coming from another direction. Chances are that trouble for him means trouble for us. Logic?'

'Bugger logic!'

She jumped up, skipped around me and headed towards the threesome's table. I was so surprised that I stood still for a few seconds and wasted more time opening my mouth to yell at her. I didn't yell, but by the time I got moving she had woven through the drinkers and had fronted up to Mal.

Mal shook his head and Erica said something loud and uncomplimentary. Mal pushed his chair back, the woman moved her body closer to him and the other guy got smoothly to his feet. He was well over a foot taller than Erica, but she stood her ground. I could feel the adrenalin starting to flow as I pushed towards the table. The minder had his hand on Erica's upper arm in an ungentlemanly grip. I came up on the side and chopped at his big biceps to break the grip. He let go and half-turned, and I swung him further off-balance by pulling on his forearm. He stumbled, and I hacked his right foot out from under him so that he fell down hard and awkwardly into his chair. He looked up, and for the first time I saw that he was very young, not much over twenty. He jumped up and threw a punch, but he wasn't set and I blocked it pretty easily.

'Real rough on women are you, son?'

Mal yelped: 'Fix him, Geoff.' Geoff tried his best, but I didn't let him get set. I gave him a short hard punch well below the belt and rasped my shoe heel down his shin bone. With the wind knocked out and a shin giving hell, most people have the good sense to sit down.

Erica flashed a smile at a man who showed some interest in joining in the action. She shook her head at him and pulled a chair up close to Mal. I leaned down hard on Geoff's shoulder and whispered in his ear.

'Don't worry, son. I'm not part of his big problem and I won't hurt him. I just want a little talk.'

He wriggled, and I put my foot down hard on his left suede shoe. Mal's face was white and I was sure I could hear his knees knocking under the table. He was looking at me with fascination and I saw that the butt of the gun under my shoulder was just visible where my jacket was open. Geoff saw it too. I closed the jacket and smiled at him.

'Just stay where you are and no-one gets hurt. You might learn something.' He nodded and I took my foot away.

Erica had pulled her chair up so close that she was almost sitting in Mal's lap. The woman with the weight problem was sitting bolt upright and trying to draw herself away from Erica as if she smelled bad. I stood up beside Geoff's chair and nodded down at Erica who was lighting a cigarette. She puffed the smoke over Mal's shoulder.

'Where's Bill Mountain?' she said.

5

'BILL who?' Mal's voice was not much above a whisper,
but his fear made the sound carry.

'We're talking about play-acting,' I said in his ear. 'About
the Bill who played Bruce Worthington in the same show
that you played Henry Majors in.'

'Christ. Who're you?'

'It doesn't matter who he is,' Erica said. 'Where's Bill,
you little shit?'

It would have been amusing in another context—four
foot whatever Erica calling a man 'little'. Mal *was* small
and he was scared, but something about the quick movement of his eyes over Erica's face and the half-head turn
to check on me told me that he wasn't dumb.

'I don't know what you're talking about,' he said loudly.
'Geoff . . . .'

'Geoff's taking a break. Listen, mate, you're right in it.
I've got a photo of you signing for a car you forgot to
return. You took your sunnies off to sign. Mistake, that.
It's a police matter if that's the way you want to play it, but
there is another way.'

'Stop yapping, Hardy.' Erica helped herself to a cigarette
from the packet on the table and did a pretty good job of
looking tough. Mal's quick, snake-like eyes moved again;
they took in her act and Geoff, who was slumped in his
chair rubbing his chin.

'What other way?' he said.

'You got Bill Mountain into the game, we know that.
Now he's missing.'

'I know he's fucking missing. S'cuse me, Glad.' Glad's
second chin wobbled as she acknowledged the apology.
She was over her fright and getting interested. She

fumbled a cigarette from what had become the communal pack and Erica lit her up. Mal watched the women sourly.

'I know he's missing. So's the bloody car. Why d'you think they're after *me?* Why d'you think I've got Geoff along, not that he seems to be any bloody good.'

'Geoff's all right,' I said. 'He's young, that's all. We have to have a talk, Mal. Here or somewhere else?'

'I don't want to talk.'

'It's me or the cops. Those pictures and the registration form with your disguised handwriting on it'll send you to gaol. And if you've been around as much as I think you have, you'll know that gaol's not a safe place if the wrong people dislike you.'

He kept his eyes fixed on my face while he felt for his drink. I moved it across for him, and he picked it up and took a sip. Glad sipped her drink too, and she and Erica puffed on their cigarettes. It was getting to be quite a cheery little party with only Geoff and me not drinking up and smoking, but then, we were on duty. Mal was doing some quick thinking.

'I might as well use you as an escort home,' he said. 'You seem to know what you're doing. If you're looking for Mountain you're looking for the car too. Right?'

'Not necessarily.'

'The car could stay missing?'

'Maybe.'

'That'd certainly help.' He finished his drink and pushed back his chair. Glad finished her drink, and Erica butted her cigarette. Geoff looked at me, and I stood up. Mal surveyed the bar carefully to see if anyone was interested in us. No-one was. He stood up and squared his shoulders, looking like Henry Majors again.

'Where's your car?'

'In the car park.'

'Good.'

He marched out; Glad tried to hang onto his arm but he shook her off. Geoff brought up the rear. Erica didn't try

37

to hang onto my arm. Mal looked nervously out at the al fresco drinkers, and hurried down the steps to the car park. We followed him to a white Holden which he unlocked. He handed the keys to Geoff.

'Where are we going?' I said.

'Woolloomooloo.'

As Glad was in an arm-holding mood I gave her mine; Erica got the idea and took hold of her on the other side.

'We'll take Glad along with us,' I said. 'What's the address?'

He gave me the street and number and I told Geoff to wait until I picked him up, to take it easy and give plenty of clear signals. Then the three of us trooped off to the Falcon where Glad waited for me to open the door like a gentleman. Erica and Glad sat in the back and lit fresh cigarettes. I started the motor which coughed a bit; I coughed a bit too, wound down my window and followed the Holden out of the car park.

'I'm shooting through,' Mal said.

We were sitting in the front room of his little studio apartment. Glad had the flat upstairs, and she'd pecked Mal on the cheek before going up. I gathered their arrangement was a convenient one for both of them, company when needed and low on demands.

Mal had made coffee in his tiny kitchen and brought it through nervously. He was older than I'd first thought, close to fifty, and, away from the pub noise and good cheer, he seemed oddly diminished, shrunken. This was despite his expensive clothes—hand-stitched shirt, European shoes—and cared-for hands. Watching him, I realised that acting a part had become an ingrained habit with him. The trouble was he switched roles a bit too often. Judgement: Mal had been a con man for a very long time, probably too long.

Any artist who worked in this 'studio' would've had to

paint miniatures. The daybed, a couple of bean bags and a low coffee table just about covered the floor space; Geoff must have slept in the bath. He bludged two cigarettes from Erica and took the portable TV off to the kitchen. I heard the sound of a fridge door, a beer can popped and the electronic babble began at low volume. Geoff hadn't contributed much to the evening, but no-one was paying him to talk.

'Before you shoot through,' I said, 'talk. My guess is you're a good talker.'

Erica sneered at the soft soap and puffed impatiently on her cigarette. Mal moved a pottery ashtray towards her and she flicked ash at it and missed.

'Can't tell you much,' Mal said.

'Tell us where Bill is,' Erica snapped. 'That'll be enough.'

'I don't know.'

'Won't do, mate,' I said. 'You must have had to deliver the cars somewhere. There must have been meetings, arrangements. That's what we want to hear about.'

'Bugger-all. S'cuse me, Miss.' He sipped his coffee. 'Instructions came by phone—where to go to pick up this and that. It's more than my life's worth to tell you where.'

'Gaol if you don't.'

'I've been thinking about that. It'd take time and there's some good legal men around. I'd have a chance that way. They might give me a break or the bloody car might turn up. If I talk I'm dead.'

'You have been thinking. Let's try to keep it general. What about dropping off the car?'

'Car park. Leave the keys, papers, all the phoney stuff. Walk away. The fee came in the mail.'

'How much?'

'Grand a unit.'

'How many've you done?'

'That'd be telling. Look, I can't help you. If I could put you on to Mountain I would. Then they could break his legs instead of mine.'

'Someone threatened you?' Erica flashed the question at him. 'Who?'

'Blower again. He put the wind up me—very nasty-sounding joker. Look, I'll play square with you; I'll tell you the only thing I know, just like I told him.'

'I'm confused,' Erica said. 'You told who?'

'The bloke on the phone.'

'Told him what?' I said.

'Mountain mentioned Blackheath.'

'Blackheath—in the mountains?' Erica grabbed at the scrap of information like the last cigarette in a pack.

'That's it. I have to explain. I hardly knew him. A few drinks and a chat. Well ....' He rubbed his thin, white hand across the lower part of his face. Then he used it to pick up his coffee cup. From the look of the hand that was about as much hard work as it was accustomed to. 'He was looking to make some money, so he told me. I'd done a few of these jobs, went all right, and they told me I could do a bit of recruiting, extra money, if I was careful. Careful! I must have been over-confident. Anyway, over a drink, he mentioned that he liked to drive up to Black-heath sometimes. That's all. I don't know why I remember it, even.'

'Any ideas on why he didn't deliver the car?'

'No. He came through all right the first time.'

'He did it before?'

'Sure. Good job. That's probably why they gave him the Audi. Shit, doesn't he know what those things are worth?'

Just talking about it seemed to be increasing the strain on Mal. For one thing, he hadn't apologised to Erica for saying 'shit'. She was hopeless at being inscrutable. Her eyes and the rapid movement of her smoking hand told me that Blackheath meant something to her, and that she was already calculating about me. I decided to show keenness by keeping up the pressure on Mal.

'You told the man who called you about Blackheath?'

He nodded. 'You bet I did. I was happy to have

something to give him. What do I owe Mountain?'

I looked at him and didn't say anything.

'It's all right for you,' he said quickly. 'I saw your bloody gun. I'm not a tough guy. I was bloody glad to have something to say to him apart from "Please don't kill me."' He finished off his coffee. 'I've had Geoff around ever since.'

'How long's that?'

'A week. What's your name by the way?'

'You don't need to know.' I stood up and rubbed the edge of my hand where hitting Geoff's biceps had hurt it. Erica stood up too.

'Where are you going?' There was a note of something like panic in Mal's voice.

'What's it to you? Come on.' I jerked my head at the door and Erica moved slowly. I started to like her more at that moment; she seemed to want to give some comfort to the little man.

'Don't you want to know what Mountain told me about himself . . . ?'

'You already told us,' I said. 'Nothing. Don't worry, Mal. You've got Geoff.'

Mal groaned but I had a feeling he could groan on cue. I opened the door and let Erica go past me.

'Say goodbye to Geoff from me and tell him to work on his balance. It's all in the balance.' I shut the door and we went down the stairs. I held Erica back for as long as it took for a quick glance along the street. Woolloomooloo is never still, never silent, but there was nothing suspicious going on within sight. Erica tottered ahead of me on her high heels and I took her arm to steer her around a pile of rubbish spilling out from a blocked culvert.

'Careful,' she said. 'That's where he grabbed me.'

'Sorry.' Her arm was thin but had some nice yielding flesh on it. It was a fine arm to hold. I opened the car and let go the arm reluctantly. I put the key in the ignition and sat back.

'Well, what do we know about Blackheath?'

She looked across at me. Her face was an interesting colour under the amber street lights. Her eyes seemed very dark and her teeth very white. 'Are you working on your car case or looking for Bill, with me?'

'It's a nice point. Does it really matter? You've got the picture now. The other people looking for him are a hell of a lot rougher than me.'

'That's true. Let me think for a minute.'

'How can you think? You haven't got a cigarette.'

That earned me a smile; she proceeded to pollute my personal space. After a few puffs, she threw the cigarette out the window. Her sunglasses had slid down across her eyes from their perch on top of her head, and she pushed them back again. They took some of the fringe up and I saw the worry line again.

'I'll do a deal with you?'

'I feel like one of your brothers again—the dumbest and littlest one.'

'I'll tell you about Blackheath if you'll come up there with me.'

'Your deals are all the same. I suppose I should be glad the terms haven't got worse.'

She smiled at me with her white teeth, and I did the best I could in return with my yellowed fangs. 'Okay. Deal. We'll go first thing in the morning.'

'No. We'll go now.'

6

I DROPPED Erica on the smart side of Centennial Park and drove home to Glebe to prepare for the trip to the mountains. It was late and I was tired, but after the suburban people-and-property work I'd been doing of late, the search for William Mountain was a change and a challenge. I put on old jeans and boots, and tossed a bush jacket into the car along with a torch and a spotlight I could rig to the battery—all probably a city man's over-reaction to the harsh demands of the country.

Erica arrived in a taxi, and slung her bag into the back seat as she got in beside me. The bag clinked.

'He might need something to drink.'

'Probably,' I said. 'So might I.'

I hadn't driven to the Blue Mountains for years, and I was surprised to see how easy they'd made it. The freeway runs you smoothly out to Parramatta, and it's plain sailing from there to the beginnings of the climb at Springwood. Erica was silent for the first part of the trip, but she opened up after Springwood and told me about life with Mountain—the drinking bouts, blocks and euphoric break-throughs that seem to be part of the writerly life. She spoke of camping trips that sounded more like fun, and filled me in on Blackheath

'There's an old house up there,' she said. 'I'm not sure who actually owns it. It's half falling down. Bill took me there to stay once. It's a great spot—clean air, you know?'

She'd created enough fug in the car to prompt a rude remark, but I resisted the temptation. I just said I'd heard about clean air.

'You get up in the morning and really feel alive. Feel like

going for a long walk, not like in the city.'

'Can you find the house in the dark?'

She looked back at the tangle of glass, metal and electrical wire on the back seat and smiled. 'You've got it all wrong. The place is in the town, not half way up a mountain. There's street lights. Mind you, there's no light in the house except kerosene lamps.' She paused, maybe to enjoy a memory. 'D'you think he'll be there?'

I blinked a few times to get rid of a momentary blindness caused by some passing high-beam headlights. 'What do I know? I'm the guy who said Mal wouldn't be in the pub tonight, remember?'

'You did a good job there though.'

It was the first bit of praise I'd earned from her. 'Thanks. We've got a few worries with this.'

She lit a new cigarette. 'You tell me yours.'

'First, why did Mountain mention Blackheath to Mal? It seems indiscreet.'

She blew smoke at the windscreen. 'And?'

'The opposition. What've they made of it? I haven't been up here for years. What's Blackheath like now—biggish?'

'No, smallish, especially now—not many holiday people around.'

'That's what I was afraid of. If the car lifters went up there to flush him out the odds are that they'd be able to do it. He's a pretty distinctive bloke, even without the big beard. What'd he be, six foot two?'

'Three,' she said. 'He's six foot three.' She fell silent after that. I thought what an incongruous pair they'd make, but of course, that could've been half the fun.

We went through Katoomba somewhere around midnight. The moon was nearly full in a clear sky that seemed to have twice as many stars in it as it does over the city. I stopped on the outskirts of the town to stretch my legs and empty my bladder. I shivered as I stood there in my cotton shirt and unlined jacket. Steam lifted pleasingly from the stream of urine. Like most city people, I like the country in small doses. The light breeze carried tree smells that evoked boyhood memories of holidays in big guest houses with stiff, cold sheets and mountainous plates of toast. I doubt if they serve that much toast these days.

From the road, Blackheath first appeared out of the blackness as a spread of lights to the right. Erica directed me around a few turns of the wide, quiet streets and down to a big corner block where an overgrown garden spilled out over broken fences on two sides. The house was set well back from the street behind high, wild hedges and shrubs that had grown to the size of trees.

I parked further down the street, and we came back quietly on foot. My boots had rubber soles and Erica wore cloth-topped espadrilles with rope soles. She also had a padded jacket, so she probably wasn't shivering as I was. We were noiseless on the footpath as we walked around two sides of the block. There were no lights showing in the house. I put my mouth close to Erica's ear and whispered: 'Where would he put a car?'

She pointed into the backyard. There was a dark hole looming beside an outhouse, which showed grey with strips of peeling paint in the moonlight. I stepped over a rusty gate, took a few shuffles through the knee-high grass and probed the black hole with a torch beam. As I switched on the torch a dog howled and I froze. It was some distance off, but the hair stood up on the back of my neck just the same. The light showed that the grass had been flattened by a vehicle and by some comings and goings on foot, but the hole, between the outhouse and what I now saw was a thick, sprawling blackberry patch, was deep and empty.

I went back to the gate and shook my head at Erica's upturned, enquiring face. Following Hardy's first law of entering strange houses at night, we went around to the front gate. It creaked open, and then we were pushing through undergrowth and straggles of privet up to the front porch. The smell from the house was so strong that it was a wonder it wasn't catchable from the street. The scents of the trees and bushes must have concealed it.

Erica's grip on my arm almost cut off the circulation. I eased her hand away, turned the knob and opened the door. The stench was like a combination of rotting meat and of a science lab in which something had gone very wrong. I'd smelled it before, in Malaya when the bodies had lain in the sun in jungle clearings and the smell of putrefaction had soaked the still hot air. This wasn't quite as bad, but it was bad enough.

The torch beam showed a long front room with a fireplace in which a fire had been thoroughly set. The furniture was standard for such places, a mixture of styles and periods, mostly sagging, all looking comfortable.

'Bedrooms.' Erica pointed to the doors off to the right and left. I looked in at the right but the double bed was undisturbed; the other room was empty, and though the smell had penetrated, neither room was its source.

'Where can I find one of those lanterns?' I realised that I was whispering, and I repeated the question too loudly. There was no need to whisper, no-one was living there with that smell. She opened another door and went down a short corridor to a kitchen that ran across the width of the house. The smell was very strong. Erica used the torch to locate a kerosene lantern on a shelf. She held it out to me and shrugged.

'I don't know how they work.'

'Give us your lighter.'

I lifted the glass, poked at the wick and got the thing lit. The light slowly penetrated the darkness and showed the outlines of the room—sink, table, bench, newspaper-lined shelves, old dresser crammed with enough cracked crockery to serve an orphanage. I inclined my head at the door at the end of the room, and Erica spoke in the same sort of whisper I'd used.

'Toilet, bathroom, storage room—there's a series of . . .' She made a sloping motion with her hands.

'Lean-tos?'

She nodded, and I opened the door and lifted the lantern above shoulder height. The kerosene smell helped a little but the stench got stronger in the bathroom and we found him in the storage room. The floor was a mess of paint tins, drop cloths, plumbing fittings and discarded machinery. He was propped up against the far wall and I heard the flies for the first time just as I spotted him. They buzzed as I kicked my way across the floor, rose in an angry cloud and settled. Erica stood stock still in the doorway; then I heard her blunder away in the dark and the sound of her retching and vomiting.

From the arrangement of the floor clutter, I decided that the body had been dragged across the floor and carefully wedged up between a wall and a heavy cupboard. Even by the dim lantern light I could see the dark smears and dried puddles of blood that marked the trail. As I got closer, there was a scurrying on the floor and a couple of rats raced for the darkness of the far corner. I came as close to the figure as I could stomach and raised the lantern. The dead man would have been unrecognisable as to features and not only because one side of the face and skull was collapsed. The rats had done a lot of work. Fingerprints were unlikely but I wasn't going to have to bother about such things or his dental history. In life he'd been of medium height and stocky build. He wasn't William Mountain.

I gave Erica the good news, if that's what you could call it, and helped her to clean up the mess she'd made in the bathroom. Then I prowled around the house trying to find out what had happened. It wasn't too hard. The man had been killed in a lean-to laundry by several blows to the head with several implements, including a bottle. Then he'd been dragged to the storage room. There was a blood-caked hammer that the flies had visited and lost interest in, along with an implement for manipulating the controls of a combustion stove and the bottle. The bottle had contained Suntory whisky.

'Who is he?' Erica fiddled with a cigarette but didn't light it.

'Don't know. My guess is he's from the car-stealing firm.'

'Bill killed him?'

'Looks that way. I'm going to go around and put things back and then we'd better get out of here.'

'Leave me the torch. I don't want to sit around in the bloody dark.' She was getting her nerve back—not that she'd done too badly anyway.

I toured the house looking for signs of Mountain's presence. There weren't many: the beds were made, the dishes had been washed, the kerosene fridge was empty and turned off. I found no road maps, no newspaper clippings or note books with indentations I could shade in and read. All I found was the whisky bottle and a book with Mountain's name in it. I took the book, put the lantern back on the shelf and we found our way out by torchlight.

Erica lit her cigarette as soon as we got through the gate.

'What now?'

'Off—as fast as we can.'

I plucked the cigarette from her fingers and took a drag, my first for years. I had to do something to get the taste of death and decay out of my mouth. The cigarette tasted like old dog blanket.

'We don't report it?'

I returned the cigarette. 'How would you like to explain what you were doing in there?'

7

WE didn't talk much on the drive back to Sydney. Erica smoked a bit and yawned a lot. At Katoomba I asked her if it was Suntory whisky she had in the bag. She shook her head, turned around and rummaged and came up with a flask of Bundaberg rum. We both had a good pull on it, me telling myself it would help keep me alert for the drive. In fact I was alert enough, but discouraged.

Car Stealers Inc. would undoubtedly go looking for their boy before long, if they weren't at it already. When they found him, Mountain would be in even deeper trouble. If he was the one who'd done the killing, his legal position looked very dodgy. The first few blows could have been in self-defence but the damage had gone way beyond that. By rights it was a police matter, but there were snags in that for me. Bring in the cops and the reporters come in the door behind them. Terry Reeves didn't need his troubles served up to everyone at breakfast along with a dash of bloody murder.

Apart from that, I felt that I owed something to Erica by this stage. She'd shown guts and persistence in her search for Bill Mountain, as well as some compassion for Mal. I liked her well enough to worry about what might go on behind that fringe now that the Blackheath tip hadn't paid off.

We were off the freeway and back into the cocoon of the inner west when she spoke up.

'Won't you get into trouble if you don't report it to the police. I mean your licence and everything?'

'Maybe. But I can handle a little pressure of that sort, or

my lawyer can. You have to make your own judgements in this business. One standover man more or less won't disturb my sleep.'

'Are you sure that's what he was?'

'Pretty sure.'

'Will you help me? Can I hire you to find Bill?'

'You can't hire me, I'm already hired. But he's still the freshest trail in this mess.'

'What will you do?'

I gripped the wheel and felt the tiredness grip me. I yawned impolitely. 'I'm too tired to think now. Maybe I can go back to Mal and squeeze some more out of him. Maybe he has a way of contacting his principals and the information I've got now could give me some leverage. I don't know.'

She huddled against the door and blew her nose violently. 'I wish he hadn't killed that man,' she sniffed. 'Why would he?'

I didn't have any answer to that, certainly not at 2.45 am. Death has a draining effect on a normal person and we were both so normal and drained that we went into my house and dumped our bags on the floor without even discussing what we were doing. I showed Erica the plumbing and the spare room, which Hilde had painted and transformed in other ways from the bare cell it once was.

'Nice room,' she said.

'Sleep tight.'

I took a pull on the rum and went to bed with the comforting warmth of the spirit in my mouth and throat.

Before dawn I woke up from a dream in which a man with a bashed-in head was following me round and round an overgrown garden. In the dream I was yelling, and I yelled for real when I stepped over a rusty gate, fell and woke up. Sweat was breaking out on my face as I sat up and instinctively looked to see if I'd woken Helen, but there was no Helen. I was half glad, half sorry for that. I lay back and waited for the sweat to dry; then I went deep under and slept without dreaming or turning over until 9 am.

The kitchen was filled with grey cigarette smoke when I got down there. Judging by the smoke and the butts, Erica had been up for a few hours. She didn't look tired as she lifted the coffee pot. I nodded and sat down wondering why I wasn't looking and feeling as good as her.

She re-charged the pot. 'Why are you looking at me like that?'

'I was wondering if Chinese people got red-rimmed eyes from lack of sleep.'

She laughed. 'I got some sleep. I feel all right. D'you want milk? There doesn't seem to be any.'

'Black is fine. The cat drinks all the milk around here. Seen the cat?'

'Yeah, it looked in and left.'

'No milk, see? Goes next door.'

We waited while the pot did its job. She poured two cups of coffee and took hers across to the sink. She leaned back against the sink and used it for a big ashtray. The morning was cool, and she was wearing a sloppy joe Hilde had left behind. It was about three sizes too big and the message 'Dentists are people too' was down around her waist. She saw me looking and tugged at the sweater.

'Does this belong to your woman?'

'No. To my ex-lodger.'

'No woman?'

'Not at the moment. She comes and goes.'

'Does that suit you?'

'Yep.'

'Why?'

'Two lives are more interesting than one.'

'Sounds like Bill's philosophy. You're a bit like him, you know. Why didn't you two get on well?'

He's more of an extrovert than me; you probably noticed.'

She smiled. 'Can we go over it all a bit? I'm sorry, I just don't know what to do.'

'Suits me.' I spilled some bread out of its wrapper and inspected it for mould. 'A talk'd be good. I need to know a hell of a lot more about him. Toast?'

We sat and drank coffee and ate toast and she talked about Mountain at length. A picture formed of a wilful, selfish man, but one capable of great emotional generosity. Erica claimed that he had taught her a lot without ever patronising her or making her feel inadequate. She thought he'd make a good teacher.

'It sounds like a gift all right, but what he wants to be is a great writer, not a teacher. How about that?'

She shrugged. 'It's what he wants, that's true. He wants it so badly.'

'Does he want it too much to do it?'

'How do you tell? I never even write a letter. I don't know what it's like to write anything. Do you?'

I shook my head.

'He reads about writers all the time. Literary biography is probably his favourite reading. He says he does it to find out how a writer should behave. When he's drunk enough . . . .'

'Yes?'

'He curses television, says real writers don't have anything to do with television.'

'Certainly didn't bother Shakespeare.'

'Don't joke; you said you wanted to know about him. Well, this was his obsession. Look.' She pulled the book I'd brought from Blackheath, and completely forgotten about, out from under the morning newspaper. 'Why did you take this?'

'I don't know. Let's have a look at it.'

The book was a thick paperback biography of Jack Kerouac. The pages were turned down at irregular intervals indicating that Mountain had read it in dribs and drabs and possibly more than once. I looked at his big sprawling signature—a firm hand that he'd tried to disguise when he wrote 'Bruce Worthington'. The date was printed boldly in figures half an inch high.

'I hope he wasn't trying to learn how Kerouac lived. He drank himself to death.'

She nodded. 'Bill wanted to stop. He tried to a few times, but he couldn't.' She pushed back her fringe and gave me an unimpeded straight look. 'Are you going to try Mal again today, Cliff? Can I come?'

I liked the 'Cliff', but I was trying to think of a way to say no, when the book came open at a page that had been turned down at the corner more than once and the binding had been strained by being bent back flat. A couple of paragraphs on the page were heavily underlined in fresh-looking ink. While Erica waited, I read the paragraphs: they described the period, late in Kerouac's life, when he went to live with his sister and tried, unsuccessfully, to stop drinking. My mind flicked back to what Erica had said about Mountain's alcohol problem.

'You said he wanted to give up the grog?'

'Yes, but he was worried that he wouldn't be able to write without it. And you know how it is, all his social contacts were drinkers, they met in pubs … he'd have to give up almost everything he did to stop drinking. It was just too hard.'

'Does he have any relatives?'

She thought about it, which meant lighting another cigarette. 'A sister, but they're not close.'

'Doesn't matter. Did he ever talk about her?'

'Mm, not much. She lives in Melbourne and she's pretty straight. Bill called her something strange, something old-fashioned. A wowser.'

'Wowser is old-fashioned?'

'Is to me. Why? What's his sister got to do with it?'

I showed her the passage in the book about Kerouac

drying out with the dried-up sister. It seemed too thin and fanciful to even be called a lead, but if I followed it I could at least get off on my own and do some investigating in my own style. My old mate Grant Evans was currently nudging his way up the police preferment ladder in Melbourne, and I could have a quiet word about stolen hire cars with him without alerting Bernsteins and Woodwards. I'd have preferred a trip to Byron Bay but you can't have everything.

'What's the sister's name, d'you know?'

'I don't know, but I know where she lives—place called Bentleigh. I remember Bill said there was no-one bent in Bentleigh.'

'Witty. She married, this sister?'

She shook her head and blew smoke over my shoulder. 'Don't think so, no.'

'That's a help. Can't be too many Mountains in Bentleigh. Is that witty?'

'Not very.'

'A terrible thought just occurred to me, Erica. His name really *is* Mountain, isn't it? It's not his nom de plume or anything?'

'God, that'd screw it up. No, I'm pretty sure it's Mountain, but I don't know why I say so.'

'I'd better go down there and see her.'

'And what am I supposed to do?'

'Why did you go to his house the other night?'

'To work through all his stuff really carefully to see if I could come up with anything. I don't know what — diary, letters—anything.'

'That's still well worth doing.'

'Meanwhile you go off doing the interesting stuff.'

I looked at my watch. 'You can come with me when I visit Mal. That's in about twenty minutes; want first shower?'

*   *   *

We were preoccupied and not cheerful on the drive to Woolloomooloo. The weather didn't help; the sky was overcast, with only pale, yellow breaks in it, and there was a swirling cold wind. The water had an ugly grey sheen, and the high buildings looked dirty against a dirty sky. I snapped at Erica when she lit her umpteenth cigarette for the morning.

'Can't you cut down on those bloody things?'

Her Oriental eyes widened, the frown line in her forehead deepened and the corners of her mouth turned down. I felt like a bully and was sorry I'd spoken, but she looked calmly at me and took a puff.

'I'll quit when you find Bill,' she said.

We walked across the street, with the wind whipping at us, to the entrance to Mal's block of flats. The building had had a sort of seedy glamour at night, but in the grey light of day it looked faded and tired. We went into the small lobby and I wondered what sort of image Mal would present in the morning. Dressing-gown? He was hardly the track-suit type; that'd be more Geoff's style.

I knocked, but there was no response. Another knock brought a slapping of slippers on the stairs behind us.

'What the hell do you want?' Glad stuck her head around the corner of the stair, looked down on us, and began an imperious descent. Her multi-coloured hair was up in curlers; she wore a violet dressing-gown with a pink sash and huge, fluffy green slippers. Splashes of high colour showed in her cheeks and her second chin quivered.

'Go away.' She looked at me with pale, watery eyes across the top of a pair of half-glasses. 'And take the little Chink with you.'

'Easy, Glad. We've come to have another talk with Mal.'

'Don't you Glad me. If you want to see him you'd better ring up the bloody hospital.'

'What?'

'He's got a broken leg and a broken arm, poor devil.

He's in St Vincent's.'

'What happened?' Erica said.

She came to the foot of the stairs and gave us the whole show—hair, dressing-gown, sash and slippers. 'They came and did him over in the early hours. I thought it mighta been you from the way you was chuckin' punches last night.'

I shook my head. 'Not me. What about Geoff?'

'Him too. In the hospital.' She nodded her head as she spoke and her glasses fell off. It had happened a thousand times before and she caught them deftly, without looking. Erica took out her cigarettes and went over to the stairs with the packet extended. Glad hesitated, then she took a cigarette and bent her head to the lighter.

'Ta. I'm a bit shaky.'

'Did you talk to Mal? Before he went to hospital.'

'Couldn't talk, they broke his teeth. He didn't think I knew he had false teeth but I knew.'

'I'm sorry, Glad.' I said. 'We'll try to look in on him.'

She nodded, pushed up her glasses and slapped her way up the stairs.

'It's hotting up,' I said.

Erica was getting the idea. She looked both ways before stepping out onto the pavement. 'It's horrible,' she said. 'Can you drop me at Bill's place?'

We drove through the tight, late morning traffic, and I thought of broken bones and hospitals, of which I'd had a bit of experience, and of Australian Chinese families, of which I knew nothing. We passed a restaurant where Helen Broadway and I had eaten, and I thought about her being physical on the farm or talking wittily on the local radio where she had a part-time job. I wondered if she'd smoked her one Gitane a day yet, or was saving it for after dinner. I wondered if she was thinking about me and thinking, as I was, that six months is a short time to have

56

something you want and a long time to be without it.

There was a mist still hovering over the park when we reached Mountain's place. The air was nearly as cold as it had been up at Katoomba, but it had a very different flavour. Erica didn't have to use her key on the front door: it had been jemmied open and pushed roughly back. It was held half-shut by the splinters.

I pushed past Erica into the front room. The furniture looked as if it had been attacked with a chainsaw—the couch had been up-ended and disembowelled. Stuffing and fabric lay around everywhere and broken ornaments and torn curtains littered the floor. Erica gave a little gasp and darted to pick something up off the floor. She clasped it in both hands and wandered through to the next room.

The chaos continued through the house and was worst in Mountain's study, where books had been dismembered and papers torn and scattered like losing betting tickets. The search hadn't been professional and the destruction looked to be the result of frustration and failure. Erica skirted around the messes—tumbled-out drawers, shredded clothes and torn photographs.

'What's missing?' I said.

'Not much. The shotgun and the car keys. Not kids?'

I shook my head. 'The TV and the VCR rule that out.'

'So it's *them*?'

'I guess so. Can we make some coffee?' We rummaged in the kitchen and found two more or less intact cups. I put on the water and spooned in the instant. Erica sat at the table and lit a cigarette. She opened her hand and let a small, gold wristwatch drop onto the pine table. The glass was shattered.

'It was mine. I left it here. Why're you looking like that?'

'Like what?'

'Scowling.'

I poured the water into the cups and added a slug to each from a bottle of Suntory that had been opened and knocked on its side so that only an inch remained. 'Bloody uninquisitive neighbours,' I grunted. 'This must have been noisy.'

Erica reached for her cup. 'Never heard them when I was here. Walls must be thick or else they're out a lot.' She sipped and made a face. 'That's not what's on your mind, Cliff.'

I drank some of the laced coffee thinking that it was a while since I'd done any spirits drinking in the morning. 'You're right. I just don't understand this. I can see the car mob wanting to get hold of the Audi. They make an investment, and it has to pay off. But this leg-breaking and house-trashing looks like something else.'

'You mean they might have found out about the man at Blackheath?'

'Doesn't seem likely. No, he must have done something to threaten them. Must've played a card of some sort.'

'What?'

'God knows. I've got to talk to Mal again.'

She nodded. She seemed to have lost drive and interest suddenly. She'd been disappointed at the pub, at Mal's flat and Blackheath, and maybe she didn't have the mule-like stubbornness it takes to keep going. Maybe it was the first violated house she'd seen; that experience takes some people hard.

'Look, Erica. There's still a job for you to do here, and I don't just mean cleaning up. Someone was looking for something and they didn't find it.'

'How can you tell?'

'I can read the signs. The destruction goes right through the place—they were angry to start with, they got angrier and they never got happy. That means they didn't find it. Your Dad can spare you from the exporting business for a while, can't he?'

She smiled. 'Importing. Yes, of course.'

'Then you can look through here inch by inch. See if you can find anything that might help us.'

'Like what?'

That was harder, but I kept myself from shrugging and looking hopeless. 'I don't know. A diary, letters, maybe some numbers written down somewhere. A phone number—anything unusual that looks contrived or done for a purpose. The only thing that worries me is that they might come back. Is there anyone you can get to come and stay here with you?'

She nodded. 'Yes, I can bring Max.'

'Who's Max?'

'He's my German Shepherd. He stands so high and he weighs about a hundred pounds.'

'Get him on the phone,' I said. 'He sounds like just the bloke you need.'

Erica said she could walk across the park to get Max. That sounded all right to me; I'd have preferred park walking to hospital visiting myself, but it seemed unlikely that the ducks and joggers would be able to tell me anything useful. I drove to the hospital and parked as near to the place as the able-bodied and non-medically-qualified could get. Then I negotiated the barriers they put between the sick and the well. They wouldn't let me see Mal, registered as Malcolm Fitzwilliam, who was recovering from a severe concussion as well as his other injuries, but Geoffrey Stafford was visitable.

They wheeled Geoff into the waiting room with the tiny, dust-shrouded windows where I'd spent nearly an hour waiting. Geoff didn't look pleased to see me; he had one leg in a cast, half an arm was in plaster and held crooked by a metal strut and both his eyes were bruised the colour of eggplant.

'What do you want, Hardy?'

'For openers, how do you know my name?'

'I did a bit of ringing around after you split the other night. With the gun and all I reckoned you'd be a private licence.' Talking was difficult for him; all facial movement would be for a while to come.

'What happened?'

'Three blokes—very quick and good, better than you.'

'That makes them a hell of a lot better than you, son. Any talking?'

'Not much, Mal didn't have anything to tell them except . . . .' He broke off and looked at me through slits in the bruised flesh. I didn't feel particularly chipper, but I must have looked in the pink to him. He gave a malicious giggle. 'Except your name.'

'He told them that?'

'Yeah.'

'And they still worked you over?'

He nodded and instantly regretted it. 'Yeah. This bloody job turned out to be tougher than it looked.'

'They often do. Did Mal say anything about the girl?'

'The slappy? No, he's a gentleman that way. He liked her, he told me.'

'What did you say?'

'Didn't get a chance to say anything. I had a go, but they fixed me up fast. I was nearly out of it, but I could just hear what was going on. What the fuck is it all about? Mal said it was a small-time gambling debt. Needed time to pay, he said. Shit!'

'Take too long to tell you. Ask Mal.' I stood up. 'What did they look like?'

He screwed up his eyes in an effort at recall and the effort hurt him. 'Three, like I said. Nothing special. Average-sized blokes, one was a bit bigger.'

'Fair or dark?'

'Two dark, one redhead.'

'Australian?'

'Didn't talk much, couldn't tell. One of the dark ones could've been a dago.'

'How's that?'

'Smell.'

'Age?'

'Not young. Thirtyish.'

I let that pass. 'Clothes?'

'Ordinary—jeans and jackets. The redhead had some gold chains around his neck. Ponce.'

'You should've grabbed them and throttled him.'

'Get stuffed.'

'Don't be like that, Geoff. You'll mend. Sorry I didn't bring any grapes.'

'Get stuffed.'

He pressed a button and a white-coated male nurse came in and wheeled him away. I paced up and down in the gloomy little room trying to assess how much worse things had got. In general, the fewer trios of efficient heavies that know your name the better. It sounded like high time for me to get myself a dog like Max or go to Melbourne.

Back home I phoned Terry Reeves and gave him an edited version of what I had. My best card was the news that one of the phoney car renters was in the hospital.

'Good,' Terry said. 'You put him there?'

'No, but he won't be driving cars for a bit.'

'Where's the one he took?'

'Sorry, mate, it's gone through the system.'

'It figures. Well, at least I haven't lost any more since I saw you. Any point in bringing a charge?'

'Not if you want to crack the system and maybe recover the cars.'

'That's the second time you've said system—how d'you see it?'

'Big operation, well-financed, good procedures, and there's something else in it—something above and beyond the cars, but I don't know what.'

'Just stick to the cars, will you, Cliff? Keep your imagination in check.'

'What about my initiative?'

'What's it going to cost?'

'I've got to go to Melbourne.'

He groaned. 'Maybe I'll take a holiday when it's all over. I need one I can tell you. Well, thanks for all the information, Cliff.'

'You know how it is—little by little.'

'Yeah, well, soldier on, Cliff, and listen, take care, all right?'

I rang off, and reflected on how much hung on this case—Bill Mountain's life maybe, Erica Fong's lungs and Terry Reeves' long overdue holiday. TAA offerred me two flights—one I could catch easily and one I'd have to rush more. I accepted the challenge, packed a bag in record time and threw in West's *The World is Made of Glass* and *The Intimate Sex Lives of Famous People.* My white jeans and shirt made me feel like a bowls player, so I put on a navy shirt and a leather jacket. I left my one funeral tie behind; I didn't expect to be visiting the Melbourne Club.

9

O<small>N</small> the plane I skipped through *Intimate Sex Lives*, jumping from the ones who'd had a hell of a good time, like Picasso and Josephine Baker, to those whom sex had made thoroughly miserable, like D.H. Lawrence and Paganini. I decided that I was somewhere in the middle. The flight took about an hour; after five minutes the woman sitting next to me clicked her tongue disapprovingly when she saw what I was reading, and stared fixedly out the window for the rest of the hour. She seemed to disapprove of what she saw out there too.

My knowledge of Melbourne is sketchy. A flight attendant told me that she thought Bentleigh was a southern suburb; I knew the airport lay to the west of the city so I took the airport bus into town. The Tullamarine freeway must be one of the most boring stretches of road on the planet; either they picked a boring landscape to run it through or they made it that way in the process. Anyway, there was nothing on the run to occupy my thoughts or delight my eye until we reached the city, which looked pretty good in the afternoon sun, if you like broad, tree-lined streets and a flat landscape.

At the city terminal I hired one of Reeves' *Bargain Renta Cars*, thinking that I shouldn't have any trouble with this item on the expense account.

'I'm sorry about all the red tape,' the woman who processed the hiring said. 'It used to be simpler.'

'That's okay,' I said. I looked for the hidden camera behind the desk, but couldn't spot it. 'Do you have a Gregory's in the car?'

'I'm sorry?'

I rapped the counter. 'My fault—Sydney born and bred. I mean a street directory.'

'There's a directory in the glove box. Where are you going, Mr Hardy?'

'Bentleigh.'

'Just look in the glove box.' Her manner became slightly distant; I was beginning to get bad feelings about Bentleigh.

The detective's friend turned up trumps with just one Mountain, initial C., listed for Bentleigh. I located the address, Brewers Road, in the street directory and headed off. The Laser was responsive and toey in ways that were just a memory to my Falcon; for the first mile I felt like a rodeo rider getting a frisky mount under control. After that, the drive out to Bentleigh was a lesson in the differences between two cities. The Melburnians seemed to have flattened large sections of the city I remembered from my last visit, more than ten years ago, and swept freeways through the clearances. That sort of thing had met more resistance in Sydney, which was just as well for me or else my living room would have been a traffic island. Also, the traffic lights were advertised as carrying concealed cameras to catch sneakers-through-on-the-red, an Inquisitional touch Sydney lacks. The camera business reminded me of the time when Melburnians would turn pale at the 'tow-away zone' signs in Sydney and our stories about retrieving cars from great distances at monstrous expense.

It was after three when I reached Brewers Road. Kids were straggling home from school, battling a wind that whipped at the tails of their raincoats and shook the trees and shrubs in the well-tended gardens. Bentleigh was one of those flat Melbourne suburbs, with the odd suggestion of a rise and fall in the landscape, which made it just possible to imagine it as a pleasant place before 1835. Now it had a solid, comfortable post-war look of brick veneer and mortgages paid on time.

I cruised down quiet Brewers Road squinting at the numbers. The woodwork on the houses looked as if it got an annual coat of paint; the road was a polite half mile from the vulgar shopping centre; there was a big Catholic church on a rise at the end of the road and not a pub in sight.

Number thirteen was a model of the sort of place that predominated in the area: broad grass strip then a low wooden fence, freshly painted, with black wrought iron gates. Neither the gates nor the fence would keep anything out or in—the rose bushes were clipped back to prevent any suggestion of them climbing on the wood—but in that neighbourhood they were de rigueur. Inside the fence was a concrete driveway and strips of concrete ran all around the edges of the lawn and the garden beds to make the whole thing easy to mow. The house was a double fronted red brick veneer set squarely on the block. The wide Australian country verandah of yesteryear had withered away to a mean little cement porch.

I parked across the road from the conventional, respectable house, and mused on the differences between siblings. In this place wild William Mountain would stand out like boxing gloves on a ballerina, but his sister evidently fitted into the environment perfectly, like the gladioli or the shaven blades of buffalo grass.

The perfect orderliness of the street was somewhat disturbed by the rubbish bins which stood in front of the houses awaiting collection. Metal and plastic with lids neatly clipped on, they were very unlike the split, battered jobs in Glebe. But there were a few plastic garbage bags and even the odd cardboard box. As I watched number thirteen, a woman came from the back of the house carrying her rubbish bin. She rested the bin on the fence and opened the gate. A couple of steps across the footpath and she put the bin down on the grass near the gutter. This put it about a metre away from her neighbour's bin which had a cardboard box next to it. The box might have

65

been sitting on the boundary line between the two properties as it appeared on the surveyor's plan. The woman looked quickly back at the houses, bent over and moved the box so that it clearly belonged in front of number eleven. I could hear the chink of bottles as she moved the box.

I watched her go back through her gate and down the driveway beside her house. She was tall, with dark greying hair and a very stiff upright stance. Bill Mountain was tall with greying hair but he had the slumped shoulders of the writer and bar-leaner.

I drove down the road, turned and came back to park directly outside number thirteen. I was in the wrong clothes to pretend to be a policeman or anything else. I took my time getting out of the car, and locked it carefully so that if she was watching she could see that I had a pride in property to match her own. I resisted the natural impulse to step over low gates; I opened this one sedately and closed it behind me. Then I walked up the carefully constructed and carefully swept concrete path to the front of the house. No bell. I took out my operator's licence with the photograph under plastic, did up the second top button of my shirt, and knocked.

She opened the front door, but left a screen door closed on a hook between us.

'Yes?' Suspicion, hostility and disappointment, all crowded into one word. Standing in the raised doorway she was taller than me which meant that she'd be close to six feet on the flat. She was wearing a cotton dress with a shapeless cardigan over it. Her face was gaunt, with sunken cheeks and eyes, and the skin around her chin and neck was scraggy. An unlovely woman. I held the licence folder up for her to see.

'Ms Mountain?'

'*Miss.*'

'Yes, my name is Hardy, I'm a private investigator. I've flown from Sydney today to talk to you.'

It can go either way—they can slam the door on you or open up and want to tell you the story of their lives day by day since continuous memory began. Miss C. Mountain looked as if she'd like to slam the door, but something held her back, perhaps the mention of Sydney or perhaps the loneliness that seemed to stand beside her like a silent twin.

'Why have you come to see me, Mr . . .', she peered at the plastic through the wire mesh, 'Hardy?'

'It has to do with Bill, your brother.'

Her right hand shot up to grip her thin left shoulder in an oddly self-protective gesture. Her voice was a dry croak. 'William. Yes.'

'Well, he seems to be missing . . . .'

'He's here. William's staying with me until he gets well.'

10

S$_{HE}$ let her hand fall from her shoulder and then clasped both hands together in front of her at waist height. She was very still and her plain, bony face and the flat lines of her body made her look like the patron saint of disapproval. There was something wrong about her stiffness, but I couldn't work out what it was. Her statement had caught me completely on the hop; I hadn't given a thought to what I might say to Mountain, because I figured the moment of meeting was days away at the earliest.

'Could I see him? Please?' I said weakly.

'He's not in at the very moment. Would you like to come in and wait? He won't be long.'

I'd picked her as the type that would send you off to your car to wait, where she could keep an eye on you from a safe distance through the venetian blinds. Wrong again, Hardy. But in this business you have to be adaptable; I put the licence away and shuffled forward.

'Thank you. Yes.'

She unhooked the screen door and stepped aside to let me pass her.

'This way.'

I was in a small, carpeted hallway that held an uphol-stered chair and a highly polished table on which sat an intricately crocheted, cream-coloured doily. A telephone sat squarely in the middle of the doily. The carpet was thick and floral, and there were plastic walking strips covering it, which led off to a room at the front of the house. I followed her down one of the strips taking care to keep my balance so that I didn't fall off into one of the bouquets of flowers.

She showed me into a lounge room that contained a glass-fronted crystal cabinet, a dresser made of the same dark wood, a couch and two chairs. A built-in briquet heater occupied one wall and the venetian blinds were half-closed to keep the light down and protect the floral carpet which flowed into here from the hallway. With all the furniture exactly in place and not a book or a magazine in sight, the room had all the warmth and welcome of a prison shower block. She stood exactly in the centre of the room, as if she had marked the spot.

'Won't you sit down, Mr Hardy?'

'Thanks.' I sat on the nearest chair so that I wouldn't wear out too much carpet by strolling around. She sat on the couch and we looked at each other in the dim light. I remembered that Bill Mountain had an engaging habit of lying on the floor, resting his glass on his chest and singing. He sang boisterously and the glass didn't usually stay on the chest. I couldn't imagine him in this room.

'How long do you think he'll be, Miss Mountain?'

She looked at her watch, which she wore with the face on the inside of her wrist. 'Oh, not so very long. He went for a walk. Would you like some tea, or coffee?'

'Coffee would be very nice, thanks.'

'It's just instant.'

'Fine.'

'Milk?'

'Please.'

'Sugar?'

'No, thank you.'

She hadn't smiled or nodded or relaxed her grim vigilant air for a second. She planted her long, thin legs in front of her and got up off the couch. With her mouth set in a tight, determined line, she marched out of the room towards the kitchen where I heard her making efficient sounds.

It wasn't the sort of room you walked about in; there

was the fear of dirt on your shoes for one thing, and the danger that you might knock something out of square. I craned forward from the chair to look at the photographs on the dresser. One was of an old, sprawling house, another showed a wedding party, pre-World War II, to judge by the clothes. The third was of a family group: the parents stood behind a boy and girl, who both looked to be about the same age, say ten. The father was a tall, angular character, closely resembling the Bill Mountain of my acquaintance and looking even more like 'Bruce Worthington' because he wore a short clipped beard. The mother was of average height and build, and would have been nondescript except that a hint of good humour about her mouth drew your eyes to her and away from the others.

Miss Mountain came back into the room carrying a tray which she set down on the dresser in front of the photographs. She held out a delicate china cup and saucer which I took in hands that felt like grappling hooks. She resumed her perch on the couch, cradled her cup and saucer in long, bony hands and let her eyes drift across to the dresser.

'The Mountain family in happier days,' she said.

'Yes.' I doubted that Bill Mountain would have thought so. The ten-year-old boy looked aggressive and resentful and the father looked exactly the same with more to be resentful about.

'Would you care for a biscuit?'

I had a biscuit and drank the thin coffee. It was almost impossible to think of anything to say to her. She sipped and nibbled and took extreme care that not a single crumb fell on the floor. The only possible topic of conversation for us was her brother, but I felt myself being irresistibly drawn into the insipid artificiality of her milieu.

'Bill's been unwell, you said?'

'Yes.' She leaned forward, but adjusted her hands so that there was no risk of upsetting her cup. 'It's a weakness, you see, that William inherited. Our father was a strict teetotaller, very strict, but Mother, well ... and the weakness came out in William. It's an illness, you understand. Mother died of it, and I'm sure it took years off Father's life. William came to me for help.'

She sat back as if she was embarrassed at having spoken so many words consecutively. It seemed like an opportunity to advance my investigation. '*When* did he come?'

'Oh, let me see ... it's been so nice having him here, getting him his breakfast in bed and making him cups of tea. Goodness, he's been drinking a lot of tea. It seems like longer than it really is—a week perhaps, or eight days. He's been going for long walks as part of the rehabilitation. He said he wants to be fit for travelling. He hasn't touched a drop, I'm sure of that.'

'Walks?' Hasn't he got a car?'

'Oh yes, it's ... somewhere.' She ran out of steam at that point and looked vague. She drank some more coffee, a little noisily I thought, and ate another biscuit. I thought I saw a faint flush in her greyish skin and the hand holding the cup and saucer trembled a fraction.

We sat. The chinks of light through the slats of the blind faded and the traffic sounds receded from occasional to intermittent and then to less than that. The oppressive cleanness and neatness of the room got to me. I wanted to smoke just to flick ashes on the furniture and to drink just to spill red wine on the carpet. The room felt as if no-one had ever cleared a throat in it, or farted.

When I couldn't take it any more I got to my feet. 'Can I see his room please?'

She stood up quickly, nearly as tall as me. 'No! Oh no, you can't!'

No point in pretending anymore. I should've been on to it sooner; people don't invite private detectives into their parlours without enquiring about their business. But her announcement that Mountain was there had taken me by surprise, probably as it was meant to do.

'He isn't coming back, is he?'

She shook her head.

'When did he leave?'

'He stayed five days. He didn't have a single drink.'

'Uh huh.'

'You say you're from Sydney? We used to live in Sydney, in Turramurra, actually. You saw the photograph of the house? That was the family home. My father left it to me and I sold it and came here.' The flush in her face mounted and her tight mouth seemed to come loose suddenly, too loose. She clasped the hands in front again as if she was trying to control the flow of words, but she couldn't. 'My father left everything to me, nothing to William. He'd just have wasted it, you see.'

I nodded, and she shivered and clasped both shoulders with crossed arms, but the words kept tumbling out. 'I'm a convert, you see. That's St Mark's at the end of the road. You saw it of course. Such a wonderful church. It's so quiet here. I like it here. Of course the house is too big for me, but I couldn't live in a smaller house.'

'No. Can you tell me why you pretended that he was still here?'

'He asked me to. He asked me to tell anyone who came looking for him that he was still here, and to keep them waiting as long as I could.'

'Why? Why would he do that?'

'Do you know William very well, Mr Hardy?'

'Not very.'

'Does he strike you as a sane, balanced man?'

'Is anyone?'

'Don't try to be funny. William . . . people say I haven't got a sense of humour and perhaps they're right, but I do know when people are trying to be funny.'

'He's an artistic man, talented,' I said. 'People make allowances for that.'

'They shouldn't; it doesn't change things. Mother was

72

said to be talented and look at what happened to her. Did you know that William was seeing a psychiatrist in Sydney?

'No.'

'He was . . . is. A Dr Holmes. He told me.'

'Do you know where he was going when he left here?'

She shook her head; the loose-cut grey hair hardly moved. 'No.'

I'd had enough of her and her house and her piety. I moved awkwardly past the dresser with its photographs and china cups, and headed towards the front door. She followed me, still gripping herself as if she was wearing a strait-jacket. The cream doily gleamed in the dim light of the hallway. I turned back to face her. She'd revealed so much that was painful, that I felt I owed her something.

'Don't you want to know what this is all about?'

'No. I'm sure it's dreadful. I don't want to hear about it.'

I put my hand on the door knob. 'I still don't see why he asked you to go through this charade.'

Her hands flopped down from her shoulders and her features tightened into a grimace that was like putting a face on mental agony. 'He said that it would be a fitting punishment for anyone who was after him to have to spend an hour with a dried-up, boring, frustrated old bag like me.'

11

I STOPPED at the first pub I came to, which was two suburbs away, and had two double scotches. I stood at the bar, looked at the racecourse picture mounted on the wall opposite, and tried to get the desperate look in her eyes and the stiff set of her body out of my mind. It was hard work. I tried to think about racehorses, and Phar Lap and Peter Pan were the only names I could recall. The barman looked closely at me when I bought the second drink. The bar was almost empty and gave the impression of not having been full since the days of six o'clock closing.

'Are you all right, mate?'

I looked at him and had trouble remembering who he was. There were seven stools lined up beside me, all empty. I sat down on one which shook with the trembling of my legs. I felt drained of energy as if I was in a low blood sugar slump, the way my diabetic mother got when she'd been on the booze for days and hadn't eaten.

'Yeah, I'm all right. Is there anywhere around here I can get something to eat?'

He told me there was a Chinese cafe across the street. I drank the scotch too fast and went out into a cool night that smelled of cut lawns, watered gardens and petrol. The pub stood at an intersection with a newsagent diagonally opposite and the cafe on the other side of the road from that. The other corner was occupied by a TAB agency. These were the first buildings I'd noticed since I'd left Miss Mountain's house with the church on the rise at the end of the road; I didn't know what suburb I was in, but it was a big improvement on Bentleigh.

Collisions with damaged lives were part and parcel of my business, but the encounter with Mountain's wounded sister had left me more affected than usual. In some terrible way she seemed to be living in her future as well as her present, and the whole thing was as sterile and comfortless as her concrete driveway. Worst of all, I felt an odd community with her, as if I was a fringe dweller on the edge of functioning humanity too. I opened the door of the cafe and confronted the sight of people in gangs and couples, drinking and eating and having a good time. I couldn't join them; I bought a couple of dishes to take away, got some cans of beer from the pub and ate and drank in the car.

When I'd eaten the hot food and put away two cans of Fosters, I felt ready to review the day's findings. It didn't amount to much: Bill Mountain had achieved some kind of an alcoholic dry-out. He had a car, maybe Terry Reeves' Audi, and he was still dropping hints and clues to his pursuers. He planned to do some travelling.

The psychiatric angle was new and disturbing. Bill Mountain was shaping as a very complex subject. I wondered what would force him to resort to professional psychiatric help if he thought he could handle as big an emotional disorder as alcoholism on his own. His treatment of his sister was another worry. For someone as fragile as she seemed to be, what he'd done was the equivalent of squashing a butterfly with an army boot. I saw her face and heard the words falling like stones from her mouth. I'd never cared much for Bill Mountain, but I liked him even less now.

I used a public phone to ring Grant Evans. Jo, his wife, sounded pleased to hear from me after all these years, which made a nice change from the receptions I'd been getting in the last few days. Years dropped away when Grant came on the line. It's a fact of modern life, local line telephone communication means more than long distance, it's half way to being in the same room. Grant's voice sounded close, comforting and familiar.

'Cliff, where are you?'

'Near a place called Bentleigh.'

'Jesus, why?'

'It's a dirty story.'

'I bet. Well, we're in Brunswick and we're expecting you right now. Have you got a Melways?'

'Yeah, I've got one.'

'You all right? Sound a bit strange.'

'I'm all right. I'll be glad to see you. Give me the address.'

I drove back to the city and through a Brunswick, steadily and surely, feeling the effects of the alcohol and not entirely sure that the Chinese food had found a permanent home. Grant's street was a shade wider, had a few more trees and contained slightly grander houses than the average for the area. Grant's house was one of the better ones, a wide freestanding terrace with all its ironwork intact, a deep front garden and a new-looking dormer window. Nothing wrong with that; Grant was a senior policeman these days with a healthy salary and appearances to keep up.

I ran my hands through my hair and blew my nose, performing a traveller's toilet before I approached the house. My skin felt dry under the stubble and my face felt asymmetrical, which it is because of the broken nose. My eyes were tired from concentrating on the unfamiliar roads, and my breath smelled of whisky and beer. It was a fine way to go calling on a friend I hadn't seen for five years, but Grant had seen me in much worse shape. He'd probably have been more worried if I'd turned up shaved and in a clean suit. And the breath wouldn't be a problem long if I knew Grant—he'd have the perfect red in stock to deal with it.

Grant opened the door and we shook hands and slapped shoulders and I went into a house that bore no resemblance to the last one I'd been in. The big terrace was warm and scruffy—the banister was hung with clothes, and books and boots littered the bottom stairs. I could hear rock music playing upstairs and a dog of indeterminate breed wandered out of a room off the hall to see what was going on.

Jo Evans is a shy woman who says a lot to Grant in private, all good sense, but not much in public. She smiled hello, and one of Grant's teenage daughters appeared at the top of the stairs to check me out. She'd left the door open behind her and the rock decibels mounted. She waved and ducked back.

'Studying,' Grant said. He shook his head in mock despair.

'Where's the other one?'

Grant looked at Jo. 'Raging,' she said.

Grant ushered me into his study. I sat down in an old armchair I remembered from his Sydney house, and he rubbed his hands.

'Great to see you, mate. What'll it be? Got some great reds.'

He looked as if he'd been sampling them more than in the old days. Grant always had a weight problem and it looked as if he'd given up the struggle. His belt was out a few more notches than it used to be, and flesh had wadded itself in comfortably around his neck and chin. He'd lost some more hair and seemed to move more slowly than I remembered, but he looked a lot happier than he had in Sydney, when he'd been trying to keep his figure neat and his hands clean.

'Give me a belt of something rough first,' I said. 'I need it. Then I'll sample your best Wimmera white.'

'Peasant.' He opened a small fridge, took out a bottle, pulled the cork out with his fingers and poured me a generous slug in a pottery mug. 'What's the job?'

I put the wine down my throat without tasting it while he used a corkscrew on another bottle. This time he filled a glass and pushed it across to me. I filled my mouth, tipped my head back and gargled.

'Jesus,' Grant said, 'would you like to mix it with dry ginger?'

'Wouldn't mind. What is it?'

'The best. Never mind. What is it that's got you looking so haunted?'

'Haunted? Do I look haunted? God, I don't know, it's a weird one. I wish I was out of it.'

'That's a change.' He sat down opposite me on a divan and sipped his red wine. I gave him the whole thing in outline; he raised his eyebrows when I got to the part about finding the body and slipping off without reporting it, but that was his only reaction. I finished my wine and accepted another. Sleep wasn't going to be a problem.

'Your focus seems to be shifting,' he said.

'How d'you mean?'

'You started out looking for Reeves' car, then you seemed to get more interested in finding this writer bloke; the way you wound up it sounds as if you're more interested in the car angle again.'

'Maybe that's just because it's your field of expertise.'

'Mm, don't think so. I'm an expert on shits, too, and this Mountain sounds like a prize example.'

'He probably is. His girlfriend's a good kid, though. Maybe I'm obliging her. D'you know anything about a racket like this? Cars going off in numbers?'

'No. Be hard to get far with that kind of thing in Victoria. Very tight at Motor Registration they tell me. Wasn't always of course.' He rolled some wine in his mouth, and let his cop's mind run. 'Insurance boys are on their toes; spray shops and spares outlets get a pretty good looking-at; stolen cars go straight on the computer and that's working smoothly. The print-outs get around real fast, even up the bush. You'd need new plates within hours.'

'Just a thought. It's bloody well-organised and must've cost a bundle to set up. Somebody must be finding it worthwhile somewhere.'

Grant drank some more red, and I enjoyed watching his enjoyment. Then he frowned in a way I'd seen before, usually when what I was doing was grossly unpoliceman-ly. 'This is tricky, Cliff. I don't know how much there is in it, but I did hear that things aren't as tight as they might be in the west.'

'Meaning?'

'You can do a bit of good with hot cars if you've got the right ones in the right places. In Askin's day in Sydney, they were shuffling licences and registrations like decks of cards. I saw plenty of it.'

'I heard,' I said. 'Nice sideline to the gambling and the drugs.'

Grant looked pained. It was an awkward moment; I'd have bet my life that he'd never taken a dollar, but the subject never sat easily with us. Usually I joked about it, but not always. The front door slammed and I heard a young female shriek followed by the clatter of feet on the stairs. Grant's face relaxed. He glanced at his watch.

'Not bad,' he said.

I lifted my glass to toast his daughter's return. 'The west you say? Could explain some things.'

'Such as?'

'I've had the feeling all along that some of the methods used have been a bit over the top. The guy up in Blackheath looked like a heavy number, and they've been breaking arms and legs. I know people do a lot for money, but if there's bent policemen involved, needing protection, that ups the stakes.'

'It's a problem,' Grant said.

'Sounds like something for this new Federal Crimes Commission or whatever it's called.'

Grant smiled.

'No good, eh?'

'How long did it take to get a standard gauge railway?'

I yawned. I was feeling the effects of the long day, and nothing Grant had said was encouraging. It sounded as if the whole case could disappear down a hole, and right then I was too tired to care. *Let it*, I thought. But I knew that I'd have to face up to Terry Reeves and Erica Fong, and I'd been down holes after things before.

'You look whacked, Cliff.'

'Yeah, I am. I'm sorry, Grant, I haven't asked you anything about how you are—the job here and all. You look happy.'

He patted his belly. 'I am. This's one of the penalties I guess. Jo's fine, the girls're good. The job's good. I couldn't fix a parking ticket here if I wanted to. I like that.'

I nodded, and he grinned at me. 'There's things I like about this place. I miss Sydney, but I sleep better here.'

'That's good, Grant. You're lucky.'

He swilled the rest of his wine. 'You're a hypocritical bastard, Cliff. You couldn't bear to do the same thing twice in a week, let alone day after day.'

I had to agree with that. I drank a little more wine and did some more yawning and things between us got easier. He told me about his plan to buy some land and make wine, and I made a crack about wine and Evans. I caught him up on the latest about a few mutual friends in Sydney, like Harry Tickener who writes for the *News*, and Pat Kenneally who trains greyhounds. I told him a bit about Helen Broadway too.

'Involved with a polygamist,' he said. 'Gawd.'

'I'm a bit of a polygamist too.'

It was his turn to yawn. 'Not much of a one I'll bet. I can't say I envy you. Anyway, I'm too old and too fat for anything but monogamy.'

It was the sort of remark you grunt at. I grunted.

'I'll fix you a bed, hang on.'

He heaved himself up, definitely moving more slowly, and went out to talk to his partner in monogamy. I sat back with the last of the wine—the polygamist, sleeping alone.

Grant came back with some bedding and plonked it

down on the divan.

'I won't tuck you in.'

'Thanks.'

'See you in the morning.'

I slept for a few hours and then had to get up and wander about until I found the toilet. Then I lay awake and read some Morris West. Then I read the 'Bigamists, Polygamists etc.' section of *Famous Sex Lives*. Eventually I put the book down and slept until I was aroused by the sounds made in the morning by people who do the same thing day after day.

Over breakfast, Grant told me he'd put an ear to the ground about the rumours on motor malpractice in the west. The older daughter Kay, the one who'd been out raging, asked Grant for money for her driving lesson, and he forked it over with an indulgent smile. Kay was the best-looking member of the family and she had the biggest smile.

'Why don't you teach her yourself, Grant?' I said.

Kay laughed. 'He gets driven everywhere, he's such a big shot. I think he's forgotten how to drive.'

Grant leaned back in his chair. 'I see myself driving a tractor in a sunny vineyard.'

'Dream on, Dad,' Kay said.

12

Evans and his offspring went to work and school respectively. As I tidied up the bedding, I realised that I had a hangover from last night's wine. Not a bad hangover, but not a thing to take up in a pressurised plane. I mentioned the fact to Jo and she came through with the sort of non-judgmental practical advice Grant had benefited from for twenty years.

'There's a spa and sauna close by that Grant uses for his hangovers. Why don't you give it a try?'

Every passing moment made it seem like a better idea; I got the address, gave Jo my thanks and went out to the car. The morning was clear and cold; I wiped moisture from the windows and finished up with a handful of grey, oily tissues that made me feel decidedly worse. The Executive Spa was a concrete building with tinted glass windows and deep carpet, even in the changing room. Another item on Terry Reeves' bill.

I hired swimming togs and ploughed up and down the little heated pool until arm weariness and boredom forced me to stop. I soaked in the spa, massaging all the working parts with the bubbles, and sat in the sauna until I'd sweated out all the toxins.

I towelled off and sauntered into the well-equipped gym. I set the Nautilus machine shamefully low and did some light work on that. Then I skipped a bit and tapped away at the heavy bag, putting more into moving my feet than my punches. The gym instructor bounced across the way they do.

'You've done it before,' he said.

'Just amateur, fair while ago.'

'You've got into some bad habits—you're opening your fist, slapping.'

I closed my fist and punched again.

He nodded approvingly. 'Where're you from?'

'Sydney. Going back today.'

He sighed. 'Jeez, I wish I could go to Sydney. Did you know that sixty-eight per cent of people in Melbourne wish they were somewhere else?'

Great place, Melbourne, you can get sociology from gym instructors.

The treatment worked. I felt so good when I got on the plane at Tullamarine that I slept all the way to Sydney.

I'd left the Falcon on an upper level of the airport car park, slotted in next to a wall. The car looked lonely now with empty spaces all around. My sprightly feet rang on the concrete and I reached, without fumbling, into the right pocket for my keys, feeling alert and competent. That's when they jumped me. Perhaps it was the restorative effects of the spa, or the gym workout or the nap on the plane, but my reactions were sharp. The first one, a big, flabby-looking guy, tried to grab me to give his mate something to work on: he got my bag swung hard into his face and then my fist driving in under the nose and up, which hurts. He bellowed with pain and backed away. That left the smaller man grabbing empty air: I brushed his wild swing away, moved in close and jolted him under the heart. He grunted and folded in two; I kept my fist classically closed and hooked him below the ear. He sighed and went down on one knee. The big man came back but I was in a crouch by then, still moving, and I came up from the crouch and butted him in the stomach. My head was hard, his belly was soft; he took the butt with all my moving weight behind it in the worst place. He collapsed, twisted onto his side and was violently sick.

We were only a few feet from my car; the blood was pounding in my head and I felt as if I could lift them both up and throw them over the parapet for a five-storey drop.

I half wanted to. Instead, I half-nelsoned the smaller man to his feet, rushed him forward and banged his face into the side of the Falcon. While he was thinking about that I opened the door and got the Colt .45 out from its clip under the dashboard.

I took a punt that the smaller man was the smarter of the two. I rolled the sick one over with my foot and showed him the gun. He was pale already and at the sight of the gun he went a bit paler. He was fat and didn't seem to have the temperament for the line of work he was in.

'Pick up the bag and put it in the car.' I jerked the Colt to underline the order and he got up slowly, bent painfully for my bag and went across to the car. He stepped around his groaning colleague and put the bag on the passenger seat.

'Now say goodbye to your mate for a while and piss off.' Another gesture with the gun and he was on his way. I'd been lucky; no-one had come up to the level while the fracas was on and he looked very lonely as he limped off down the ramp. I couldn't expect the luck to last, so I swung the gun around and dropped onto my knee beside the other man. We were sheltered behind the car and he looked very scared.

'Get in the car,' I said. 'Do everything right and you still have a chance.'

He swore, to give himself courage, but he got into the car. As I got in, a car roared up the ramp and into a space a few metres away. I looked at my companion; he had an acne-scarred face, sparse lank hair and an expression that suggested he was out for revenge against the whole world. If I'd been drawing up the battle orders I'd have sent him in ahead of Flabby. All things considered, he'd recovered pretty well from the battering he'd had; his wind was coming back and he was working on it, taking medium deep breaths slowly.

'It's pretty quiet here,' I said. 'I've got the windows up as you see, and I can wrap something around this. I can put a bullet in you anywhere I like.'

The new arrival slammed his door and went over in the direction of the lift. The noise was muffled, almost squishy in the closed car.

'Hear that? The bullet that cripples you can make less noise than that. Understand?'

He nodded and took a slow breath.

'You can stop working on your wind; you've been out-classed; accept it. Now if you want to walk away from here you're going to have to do some good talking. I'm going to have to be pleased with what you say.'

He nodded again and didn't move his diaphragm.

'You're in with the people who're nicking the cars?'

'Sort of.'

'What does that mean?'

'I know who you're talkin' about. I've heard of them. But there's a couple of ... there's people between me and them, like.'

'What were you supposed to do here?'

'Get you to tell me where the tapes and the film was.'

'I'm not with you.'

'That's all I bloody know—tape of a voice on the phone and a fuckin' film.'

'What sort of film?'

'I know what's on it, that's all. There's a bloke gettin' into a car and drivin' away. That's all.'

'And I'm supposed to have these things?'

His bitter look got more bitter, and I moved the gun a fraction to remind him who held the cards.

''s right. Yeah.'

'Next question—who's the man you go through? Don't worry about him going through someone else.'

He shook his head. Although he was over thirty, some of the acne scars had an angry recent look as if the condition was occasionally still active. 'No way. I'm a dead man if I open me mouth on that.'

'You could be dead if you don't, or worse.'

He looked at me. Now that he'd recovered from his belting and fright he looked intelligent under the anger, intelligent and maybe capable of judgement.

'Bullshit. You won't do a thing. I'm going.'

He lifted the locking button, opened the door and slipped out. Moving slowly away he stuffed his shirt back into his pants, hunched his shoulders and walked. He'd judged me accurately; I watched him go—moving loosely, indifferently, almost strolling and without a suggestion of a backward look.

He looked better than I felt. The adrenalin rush had stopped, leaving me feeling drained and feeble. It was something they warned us about in Malaya and something well-known to the snipers. More men died in the post-battle, let-down period than in the heat of the fight. I started the car and warmed the motor properly; I put the gun on the seat and wound down both front windows for better visibility. Sensible precautions against my attackers having another go, but what I really wanted was a quiet drive home and a steadying drink.

The quiet drive I got, but not the drink because every bottle in the place had been smashed and the wine cask had had a carving knife put through it. The mess upstairs included a cover ripped from my foam mattress, lifted carpets and the overturning of everything that had stood on legs. Books and papers were torn and scattered around and the contents of drawers and cupboards had been emptied out and sorted through with a claw hammer. The technique had been much the same as at Mountain's— more of a rummage than a search, more of a destructive rampage than a teasing out of hiding places. The work on the bottles and cask was pure malice, reaction to the inevitable failure of the visitation.

I started cleaning up in a haphazard fashion and my mind ran on the obvious track until I came across two sound cassettes that had had their tapes drawn out and cut and my three video cassettes that had been pulverised by a hammer. I mused on taped telephone voices and film of a man driving away in a car. Secret service, undercover stuff. I left the mess and made instant coffee as an aid to thought.

He wouldn't tape his instructions, film the pick-up and use the material to put pressure on the firm, would he? Then I remembered the conversation Erica Fong and I had had about Mountain and I grabbed the phone which my visitors had left intact. There was no answer at Mountain's number or at the one listed for E. Fong in Bondi Junction. Centennial Park, who are they kidding? The phone book tells it like it is. I stood in the mess and heard the phone ring ten times. Maybe she'd taken Max for a walk in the park and had got into a deep and meaningful with Patrick White.

I hung up wishing for about the hundredth time that I could be dealt out of this game. I didn't like my cards and I didn't like Mountain. Erica would be better off without him. Maybe I could tackle the job for Terry Reeves in another way. Then I saw something on the floor I hadn't seen before. Helen had given me a copy of *The Macquarie Dictionary* to resolve our frequent disputes about spellings and pronunciations. The book had been dismembered; pages had been torn out and crumpled and the covers had been ripped from the broken binding. That made it more personal.

I kept ringing Erica as I finished tidying up and throwing things away. I told myself the place had been getting too cluttered anyway. Force of habit took me out to the letterbox which is hidden in a place in a hedge by the front gate known only to the postman and me. I took the priority-paid envelope out and went back into the house, wondering if the ransackers had found the miniature bottles of Jameson's Irish whisky Cy Sackville had given me, souvenir of a legal conference in Dublin. They hadn't;

the little bottles nestled behind the biscuit tin that hadn't had any biscuits in it since Hilde left. I got the foil top off and poured the small measure over a couple of ice cubes and silently toasted my Irish ancestors.

The writing on the envelope was unfamiliar. I thumb-nailed it open and took out a couple of photocopy pages and a sheet of tinted, lined notepaper. In a round, young hand Erica Fong had written:

> *Dear Cliff,*
> *I've gone to Nice to try to find him. I got the postcard two days ago. I looked through the house very thoroughly but all I could find was some notes about seeing a psychiatrist. I enclose copy of the postcard and the notes and I'll get in touch as soon as I find anything out.*
>
> *regards,*
> *Erica F.*

Mountain's two quarto pages of single-spaced notes were perhaps unique in psychological literature. They took the form of an account of the analytical session from the patient's point of view and included phrases like, 'Dr Holmes appeared ill at ease' and 'Holmes has built a house of fantasy upon foundations of illusion.' I put the notes aside for closer study later and picked up the other sheets which were copies of both sides of a postcard.

The picture showed a large city square at night. The roads were busy and the pavement cafes were thronged. On a building more or less centred in the picture, the words 'Hotel des Anges' were mounted in neon. The card was undated and addressed to Erica Fong. It read:

> *Dearest Fong,*
> *I am here to check a few people out, including myself. I haven't had a drink for more than a week and the world's not as I thought it was—much worse.*
> *A bientot, my dear little slappy,*
>
> *B.*

The 'B' was written in the large sloping hand of the notes, but the message on the card was typewritten. I took the photocopied page across to a lamp and studied it under light. There was a slight line around the text that didn't seem to be part of the card. Conclusion: the message had been typed on a piece of paper which had been stuck onto the card. I didn't have the faintest idea what this piece of deduction meant, but I was pleased to have worked something out. I was also glad that Erica Fong wasn't hanging around Sydney somewhere to be visited by people with hammers looking for tapes and films.

I sipped the Jameson's and tried to recall what I knew about Nice. Not much. Cary Grant and Grace Kelly in *To Catch a Thief*; Graham Greene wrote about a corrupt mayor; nice beach, they say, and someone named a biscuit after the place. I hadn't eaten for some hours and I was feeling the effects of the Jameson's just a little; that was alright with me. I opened the other bottle to feel the effects some more; there's more in those titchy bottles than you think. What else did I have to do? I was sitting in my ransacked house waiting for a Chinese girl to tell me what she'd found out in Nice. *Bizarre, Hardy*, I thought. *Bizarre*. Then the phone rang.

'Cliff Jameson,' I said.

'Oh, God, Cliff. It's Helen. Are you drunk?'

'No.'

'Where've you been?'

'Nowhere.'

'What do you mean, nowhere? I've been phoning for a day.'

'I mean nowhere—I went to Melbourne.'

'Oh, sorry. Are you alright? I've been missing you.'

'Me too. You, I mean. D'you like polygamy?'

There was a pause and then her voice contained a note of caution. 'It's all right, it's better than celibacy. You're not being celibate, are you?'

I grunted. 'It's been a funny day. I've won a fight and

89

now I have to clean up my house.'

'I'm glad you won the fight. Well, I just wanted to hear your voice. I'm fine of course, thanks for asking.'

'I'm sorry, love. I'm in the middle of a shitty case. I can't see the tunnel, let alone the bloody light. Have you ever been to Nice?'

'Yes.'

'Nice?'

'Don't. That joke is prehistoric. Yes, it's great—good beach, you'd love it. Are we going?'

'Maybe. You know a big square there, lots of traffic?'

'Place Massena it sounds like. What's all this about?'

'I wish I knew. How's the farm and the radio station and the winery and the daughter?'

'Don't be bitchy, Cliff. I can't help it if your life's an empty shell without me.'

'I miss you, that's all. First month's the worst. By the fifth month Helen'll be just something to go with Troy.'

'Huh. What've you been reading?'

'*The Intimate Sex Lives of Famous People.*'

'I've read that. Who d'you like best?'

'Bertrand Russell.'

'Why?'

'I like him best at everything. Who's yours?'

'Guess.'

I guessed and didn't get it right and we laughed. It went on like that for a while until she was so real to me again that I felt I could reach out and touch her. It was a good feeling. I had nothing but good feelings about Helen Broadway. I wondered how good old Mike and the kid would feel about a three month rotation.

●

13

I SPENT the rest of the afternoon re-stocking the fridge with fluids and solids. I bought some glasses and coffee mugs to replace the broken ones. I scotch-taped some books together and tidied up papers. The cat came home, got fed and went off again. I was moping and I knew it. I sat down with a pen and pad and some wine and tried to do some constructive thinking.

The results didn't justify the amount of wine consumed. My brain felt slow and tired as if something connected with the Bill Mountain affair impeded its proper engagement. My thoughts kept drifting off onto other subjects, like Nice, the Melbourne gymnasium, Helen Broadway's nose. In the end, after writing down the names of all the people so far involved and connecting some of them with arrows and covering a lot of paper with question marks, I gave it up. I decided to sleep on it, which sometimes brings results.

In the morning I had my results. Three thoughts had taken form: one, I could locate Mountain's psychiatrist, Dr Holmes, and pump him; two, I could ask around about the men who'd attacked me in the car park and try to find out who they worked for; three, I needed to find a spa and sauna in Sydney—beating two men in unarmed combat had made me a convert.

Dr John Holmes' rooms in Woollahra were in a road that seemed to be shooting for the 'most leafy stretch in Sydney' award. It was all high brick fences with overhanging trees; trees along the footpath, trees on a central strip dividing the wide road, trees waving up around the tops of the lofty houses. It cost big money to get a lot of leaves to rake in this neighbourhood, and Holmes had to be coining it—his brick fence was one of the highest and his trees were among the leafiest.

I parked outside Holmes' place under a plane tree and reflected on how very differently people go about their business. I was here two days after I'd had the idea to come. Me, you can just ring up, and like as not you can come over and see me or I'll come to you. Or, if you happen to be in St Peter's Lane, you can walk through the tattoo parlour, romp up the stairs and knock on the door. Not so with Dr Holmes. I'd been given fifteen minutes. There were no free evenings, no lunches, no half-hour before the busy day began. It sounded obsessive to me. I imagined a pale, pudgy creature, eyes luminously intelligent with legs ready to drop off from disuse.

I pushed open the iron gate in the high fence and walked up the leaf-strewn path to the front door. The house was a wide, towering affair, built of sandstone blocks one size down from those used in the pyramids at Giza. It had gracious lines—bay windows, and a wide, bull-nosed verandah over an ornately tiled surface that swept away around both sides of the house.

The doorbell was answered by a tall, slim woman wearing a white silk shirt and jodhpurs. She had a mane of blonde hair and high, expensive-looking cheekbones. Her blue eyes were elaborately made up with long dark lashes that fluttered like car yard bunting.

'Mr . . . ?' she said.

'Hardy.'

'Oh good. I think he's ready to see you. I'm going riding.'

'Not yachting?'

'A joke. I don't like jokes. D'you think I look right?'

She backed off; I stepped after her into an entrance hall big enough to canter horses in. She rotated slowly in front of a three metre square mirror.

'Umm,' she said. She seemed to have forgotten who I was, in the ecstasy of self-admiration.

'Hardy. To see Dr Holmes.'

'Oh, yes. You go up the stairs and it's the first door on the right or left. I can never remember which but you'll be all right because there aren't any doors on the side it's not on. 'kay?'

''kay,' I said.'

I went up a few stairs and turned back to look at her. She was standing by the door peering out through the peep hole.

The stairs were covered in deep blue carpet and the banister rail was polished, old and grooved and a pleasure to lay your hand on. Like all the best staircases it had two flights with a flat central section at the turn—on these it was about the size of a boxing ring. The door was on the right if you were going up but on the left if you were going down—perhaps that was what had confused the lady in the jodhpurs. I knocked on the door and went inside when a deep, pulsating voice told me to.

The man standing behind the big desk was forty plus, six feet tall with bushy dark hair and a fairways and nineteenth hole complexion. His bulky, still spreading body, displayed in a blue and white striped shirt and grey trousers, owed more to the nineteenth hole than the fairways. He reached across the desk and we shook somewhere in the middle of the vast polished expanse. Strong grip.

'Sit down, Mr Hardy, I can't give you long.'

I thought he stressed *give* the way a man who charges a fortune by the hour might, but I could have been wrong. 'This won't take long. Doctor.' I'd noticed the leather couch as soon as I entered the room but I was careful to avoid even touching it. I sat in a matching leather chair. The chair seemed to have been made exactly for the comfort of my often-stressed back. It immediately relaxed me which made me immediately wary.

He picked up a pencil. 'What can I do for you, Mr Hardy?'

His voice was one of the best I've heard, rich and rewarding. If this voice gave you the news that you were dying of cancer it wouldn't feel so bad.

'I gather you haven't come to see me in my professional capacity.'

'No, more in mine, although I guess that's semi-professional.'

He smiled showing the strong white teeth I'd have expected. 'You're defensive.' He looked down at a note pad and touched it with his pencil. 'A private enquiry agent. Interesting activity?'

'Occasionally. Your professional path has crossed with my defensive semi-professional one—you have a patient named William Mountain.'

He nodded; on his scale of fees that was probably a ten dollar nod. It forced me to go on.

'I need some information about him.'

A shake of the head—another ten bucks.

'Or at least your opinion.'

'I can't discuss my patients with you, Mr Hardy. How could I? This is the most confidential branch of the medical profession as you must be aware.'

'I doubt that it's more confidential than mine though. Maybe it is. Let's see. Maybe we can trade confidences.'

'I doubt it.'

'I leaned forward from the too-comfortable chair across the table. The table had a beautiful surface and some padding around its edges, like the good doctor. 'A few days ago William Mountain beat a man to death using, among other things, a bottle. This is known to me and a very few other people. It is not known to the police. Can you get more confidential than that?'

His big, fleshy lips pursed and he ran a broad, capable-looking hand through his bushy hair. 'Are you sure of that?'

'Are you surprised?'

'Not really.'

'Well, that tells me something. You think he's a dangerous man?'

'You can't outfox me, Mr Hardy. I'm not going to confirm your guesses.'

'Look, I'm not here to play word games. I'm trying to find this man. He's in bad trouble and he needs help. His girlfriend wants to help him. I'm more concerned about other things, but I've seen some of the harm he's done and I don't only mean physical harm.'

That got a lifted eyebrow. No charge.

'I think it's better that he doesn't do any more harm. There are two paths ahead of him—one leads to court and the other to the crematorium. Believe me. Either way you're going to be called to talk to the authorities. If he gets a bullet in the head, it could be your fault for not talking to me now.'

'You're persuasive, Mr Hardy.'

'I'm trying to be. I'm also telling you the truth.'

'I believe you might be. Who would kill Mountain?'

'Criminals, obviously.'

'Why?'

'He's involved in something big and dirty. He's being foolish. He's threatening people who don't know about turning cheeks.'

'It doesn't surprise me.' He leaned back in his chair and then came abruptly forward. 'Do you mind if I smoke?'

'They're your lungs.'

He got a long thin cigar out of a drawer, unwrapped it and lit it with a gold lighter. The smoke went down into his barrel chest and came out in a thin hard stream that floated up towards the extravagant ceiling rose. With the cigar in his hand and framed against a big window that ran from knee height almost to the ceiling, he looked like a wrestler on his day off.

'William Mountain is a very disturbed man. It's hard to

give a name to his central problem. You could call it an identity crisis but it would take a very broad definition of the word "identity" for that to cover it.'

'Can you predict a likely outcome?'

'To what?'

I gave him a summary of Mountain's movements and actions; he drew on his cigar and listened patiently. I held back on the notes Mountain had kept on his sessions with Holmes, because I thought of that as a card I could play if I needed to. When I finished he sat quietly and puffed smoke. I assumed he was thinking, and God knows what his rate was for that. I let my eyes travel around the room taking in the bookcases with the glass fronts, the slimline electric typewriter on the desk and the Impressionist paintings on the walls. He stubbed out the cigar in an ashtray which he put back in the drawer he'd taken the cigar from.

'It's very difficult,' he said melodiously. 'I wish I could talk to him.'

'Me too. Is he a likely suicide?'

He spread his hands non-committally.

'What would you be advising him to do if he was here now?'

'I don't advise. I listen.'

'Jesus, you're doing pretty well out of listening.'

'Don't be offensive.'

For no good reason I looked again at the elegant typewriter on Holmes' desk. I was letting my mind run free on the subject of Mountain, who had no doubt lain on the couch a few feet away and told Holmes a lot of things, some of them things it could be useful to know. I wondered if Holmes typed up his notes and where he kept them. Holmes followed my gaze. He looked impatiently at his watch.

'Mr Hardy . . . .'

I got up and took a closer look at the typewriter. It had a sheet in it with a couple of lines of typed verse about a red knight and blue blood that didn't mean a thing to me. The typeface looked very similar to that on Bill Mountain's postcard.

'This is a super-portable, isn't it—for travelling?'

Holmes sighed. 'Yes.'

'Mountain wrote a note on a slip of paper and stuck it to a postcard. I thought he might have pecked it out in a shop but these cost a mint; they don't leave demo models around.'

'What's your point?'

'Mountain's got a traveller's typewriter, expensive one. Means he expects to be writing.'

'He's a writer, isn't he?'

'Yeah, but he was totally blocked. He was obsessed with writing a novel; he couldn't write it and it was eating at him. Right?'

Holmes nodded. 'One of his obsessions.'

'If he was actually writing this book, would that make a difference to him, to his behaviour?'

'Conceivably. If it went well it could absorb him, calm him down. If it went badly it could push him in any direction.'

'What if it went well and he managed to stay off the grog?'

'That's unlikely. Alcohol is one of his favourite, I might say most cherished, obsessions. And in case you think you've opened me up, I'd point out that Mountain is on the public record about that.'

'Mm. But just say he was sober and writing well?'

He put the capable looking hands on the desk and examined them as if he'd never seen them before. Then he looked at his watch.

'I've got an appointment. I expected you to be some dim summons server, Hardy. I can see that you are not.' He smiled and put a lot of warmth in it; the smile and the voice together would bowl over most women and a lot of men. 'In fact I think you have a genuine interest in human character which is quite an unusual thing to have. So I will take a chance with you. This is a complete shot in the dark, but I'd say that if Mountain managed to achieve the sort of self-control you're talking about he would be capable of extraordinary things—a great novel, a terrible crime. Almost anything.'

I stood up and he stood too. We were about the same height as we faced each other over the antique desk. I guessed he would get a lot of transference from his patients—that process where the progressing patient imagines that he or she is in love with the analyst. Hilde used to say that it happened a bit with dentists, too. It wasn't a problem I'd had to contend with. He came around the desk to see me out and we shook hands again.

I couldn't resist it; he was just too comfortable and secure for my liking. 'Did you know that Mountain kept notes on his sessions with you, Doctor? He analysed you, spotted a few weaknesses too.'

His grizzled, pepper-and-salt eyebrows shot up and he looked positively pleased. 'Really! How interesting. But I can't say I'm at all surprised. I recommended just such an activity as part of his therapy.'

14

I DIDN'T see the woman in the jodhpurs on my way out, but I did recognise Dr Holmes' next patient as I passed through the gate a little ahead of him. Anyone who watched television or read the tabloids would know him from his talk show, where he smiled equally broadly at beauty queens with impoverished vocabularies and RSL officials emotionally arrested in 1945. He was never heard to voice an opinion and was known for his unflappability. He looked pretty flapped now as he advanced towards Holmes' doorway, as if he was about to melt under the strain of all that affability. I greeted him by his Christian name and he shot me a look as haunted as any ever dreamed of by Edgar Allan Poe.

I drove to my office where the only thing happening was the gathering of dust. On the way back to my car I stopped in at the tattoo parlour on the ground floor, to try out the descriptions of my car park playmates on Primo Tomasetti. Primo has a photographic memory for the faces that sit on top of the bodies he tattoos.

There was no hum coming from the shop, which meant that Primo wasn't working. I knew he'd either be dozing or sketching designs for tattoos, designs that would always owe a lot to Goya and William Blake. I pushed aside the curtain and saw him hunched over his cartridge paper with a crayon held in his thick fingers moving rapidly in bold strokes.

'Where d'you get your inspiration from?' I said.

Primo looked up and grinned. 'It's in the blood.' He scratched at his wiry black hair and brushed the shoulder of the white lab coat he wore over a pink shirt. I once told him he should put a row of ballpoints in the pocket of the coat and he'd look like Ben Casey, but, like everyone under forty, he's never heard of Ben Casey. 'My grandfather was the greatest document forger in World War I.'

'On which side?'

Primo scratched some more. 'I never bothered to ask. Does it matter?'

'Not for World War I it doesn't. Look, Primo, I ran into two unfriendly guys the other day—one big, flabby, bit slow, the other was smaller, dark with a bitter look, like he'd gone straight from the orphanage to Long Bay. Ferrety-looking. Any ideas? They seemed like a team.'

'Hard to say, Cliff.' He put down the crayon. 'Can't place the flabby one, he sounds like ten cops I know. What's a ferret?'

'Small animal they put down holes to flush out rabbits.'

He picked up the crayon and a rabbit appeared on the paper.

'That's fascinating. What happens next?'

'You shoot the rabbits when they come out or wring their necks. I had an uncle used to do it. He'd ride for miles on his bike and he'd always bring back a bag of rabbits.'

'Did he bring back the ferrets?'

'Yeah, in a cage on the back of the bike.'

'What did he send down after the ferrets to get them out of the hole?'

'I don't know.'

'Strange place, this Australia. Weird customs. Okay, a guy who looks like he could go down holes after rabbits. That sounds a bit like Carl Peroni.'

'He didn't look Italian.'

'Not all Italians look like Al Pacino. Some in the north look like Robert Redford. It sounds like him is all I'm saying.'

'Where does he hang out?'

'Mostly in a coffee place with a pool room called the

Venezia. Off Crown Street, you know it?'

'I think so, yeah. Thanks, Primo.'

'Hang on, Cliff. I'd go very quietly there if I was you.'

'I'm known for my tact.'

'Seriously.'

'I'm not planning to bust the Mafia, mate. I'm just going to show the flag, show that I know who works for who and how to find them.'

'What good would that do?'

'Always helps to be positive—attack the net.'

'Attack the net. Is that how they catch the ferrets?'

'No, that's tennis. If I find out how they catch the ferrets I'll let you know, seeing you're so interested.'

'You could ask you uncle.'

'He's been dead for twenty years.'

Primo starting hatching in a section of his drawing. 'That probably means his ferrets are dead, too.'

Being mono-lingual, I'll give the last word any day to a man who can make a joke in his second language. Besides, doing that usually makes people happy to talk to you again and Primo was a first-class source.

It was after five, getting towards wine or gin time rather than coffee time, but I wandered down to the Venezia anyway. It was a nice afternoon for a walk, or would have been sixty years ago when my rabbitto uncle was a boy. Now the traffic was banked up in William Street right back to the tunnel. The air was thick with fumes from idling engines, the case for lead free petrol seemed urgent.

I was wearing a white shirt, dark pants and my Italian shoes; I could play a fair game of pool but my Italian was non-existent beyond *una cappuccino molto caldo, per favore*. The Venezia has two entrances, one on one street and the other around the corner which is occupied by a florist. From the steady twenty-four-hours-a day, 365-days-a-week trade the Venezia did, you'd have thought they could've bought out the florist and expanded, but maybe the florist didn't have a price. I wandered in at Crown Street, bought my coffee and went through pinball and video game purgatory to the pool room. You could buy coffee in there and something stronger if you had the right look about you. All four tables were in operation and the couple of nests of tables and chairs were crammed full of men talking, sipping and smoking; no women. I leaned against the counter and watched a player run a series of balls into the pockets. He had the expert's simultaneous total concentration and relaxation—whether he'd have grace under pressure was another question.

I finished the coffee and ordered another. The man serving it wore long sideburns that covered his cheeks to within a centimetre of his nostrils. He wasn't busy but he seemed determined to give me the minimum attention he could get away with. I fumbled for money and counted it slowly to extend his attention span.

'Do you know Carl Peroni by any chance?' I compared a dull dollar coin to a shiny ten cent piece.

'Carl? Yes.' His fingers obviously itched to pull the right money from my handful of coins.

'Expect him in tonight?'

His shrug sketched the coastline of the Bay of Naples in a single movement. I got out a ball point pen and flicked it; I really had his attention now.

'Got a bit of paper? I want to leave him a message.'

He pushed a cardboard coaster across the counter towards me. I gave him the right money for the coffee and added the dull dollar. On the coaster I wrote: 'Enjoyed our meeting in the car park, Carl. We must do it again sometime.' I added my name and the office phone number. The counter man craned forward to read it. I pushed it across.

'Give it to him, will you? And buy him a coffee.'

He looked out into the cigarette fug; the air was as blue as in William street and we had the noise of the mechanical

102

and electronic machines instead of the cars. 'Could be in later,' he said.

'I'm busy. It's not important.' I finished the short black in a gulp and walked out. The florist was just closing; I stood on the pavement and watched him pull the street displays in and tidy the shop. He was a tall, thin, middle-aged man wearing a dust coat and a bow tie. He whistled while he worked. I remembered that it was one of the many complaints of Cyn, my ex-wife, that I never bought her flowers. It was true, I hadn't. I tried to a couple of times after she first mentioned it, but I could never feel right about doing it. I wondered what Dr Holmes would make of that.

I'd given Erica Fong a key to my place before sending her off to stay at Bill Mountain's house with Max. I was glad that she'd used it and glad she was asleep on my couch. I was in the lonely mood my work sometimes brings, a feeling that other people are only contacts, sources of information or problems, and I needed to talk to someone who was more than that.

She was sleeping quietly with her straight hair all spikey and her head resting on a pillow she'd made of an expensive-looking leather coat. One hand, the nicotine-stained one, was under her head and the other was curled in a tight fist as if she was ready to throw a punch the instant she woke up.

Two bottles of duty-free Scotch poked out of the big overnight bag by the couch. I guessed that at least one of the bottles was for me so I took it out to the kitchen, got rid of all the cardboard and wrapping and poured a hefty slug of it over Australian ice. I had a mouthful to make sure the stuff had travelled okay, and then took the bottle, some ice and another glass back to the front room.

She didn't look travel-stained and I suppose that's one of the advantages of being small. An airline seat, especially a first class one, would allow enough room for reading, eating and drinking, and isometric exercises. A brush of the teeth, nothing to shave, and you're right. Erica was wearing fashionably baggy pants and a loose cotton top. Her espadrilles were on the floor and I noticed that she had the shapely feet only small women have. There was a carton of Benson & Hedges cigarettes in the bag and another open on the arm of the couch. I had to conclude that either she wasn't a woman of her word or she hadn't brought Bill Mountain back with her.

She stirred briefly and came awake quickly. She sat up, stretched and reached for the cigarettes.

'Hi,' she said. 'I just got in. I dropped off.'

'You're entitled, flying however many miles it is in however few hours.' I held up the Scotch and she nodded. I made her a drink while she inhaled and exhaled as if that's what life was all about. When she had tried her drink she looked at me gravely.

'I didn't find him.'

'I'm sorry.'

'I spent Dad's money like a lunatic just getting around. Everything costs the earth ... .' She broke off the travel chat for more alcohol and nicotine and when she spoke again the worry line was like a small fold on her forehead. 'It looks bad, Cliff. I don't suppose you ...?'

I shook my head.

'I bought a bottle of Scotch for you and one for him, just in case.'

'He's stopped drinking.'

'He's what? How d'you know?'

'I saw his sister in Melbourne.'

'I shouldn't be surprised. He's doing some crazy things.'

'Like?'

She finished her cigarette and lost interest in her drink. She tucked her legs up under her and folded her arms and looked like a sad Oriental statue. 'It's weird, let me tell you,' she said. 'I went to Nice, flew there with just one change. I can't speak any bloody French but I showed the taxi driver the postcard and he took me to the hotel. It's run by this amazing woman with long black hair and diamond rings. She speaks good English and she's got a big dog, a Doberman. We big-dog people get along. Well, I had a photo of Bill and I showed it to her and she said he'd stayed there for a couple of days. He'd arrived from Marseilles.'

'What was he doing in Marseilles?'

'I think he was buying heroin.'

'Jesus. Why d'you think that?'

'Madame at the hotel—she said she saw Bill down at the beach sitting in a chair talking to a bloke. She says this bloke is a well-known Marseilles heroin dealer. They set the deal up in Marseilles and deliver in Nice. Don't ask me why. They have all these chairs lined up on this concrete promenade . . . .'

'I've seen it in the movies.'

'It's lovely, and you could talk privately there. I mean, not be overheard. Oh God, Cliff, he's never had anything to do with hard drugs. I'm sure of that.'

'I don't think he'd be in it to play around with the stuff himself. Go on, what else did you find out?'

'He talked to Madame a bit, in French. He speaks good French—*she* said it was good, and they don't go in for that sort of praise much, the French. I said sil voo play and got laughed at. Anyway, he went to Antibes and a place called Cap Ferrat. Want to know why?'

I thought about it while I worked on my whisky. I was getting ready to take over her abandoned one too. Cap Ferrat—easy—Somerset Maugham lived there for years. Antibes—something to do with Picasso? Then I remembered the paperbacks in Mountain's study—the foot or so of orange-covered Penguin editions of Graham Greene. Graham Greene lived in Antibes.

'Somerset Maugham and Graham Greene,' I said. 'He went to look at their houses.'

She almost dropped the new cigarette she was fiddling with. 'That's right! That's right!' She lit the cigarette and didn't protest when I took over her whisky. 'How did you know that?'

I waved her smoke away airily. 'Nothing to it; you say Arles you mean Van Gogh, you say La Jolla you mean Raymond Chandler.'

She looked at me through the haze. 'You *are* like him, that's the sort of trick he could do.'

'Go on. He went to look at a couple of writers' houses. Then what?'

'Then nothing. He told Madame that's what he was doing. He watched TV with her and he fucked her.'

'She said so?'

'No, but I could tell, just from the way she looked, the way she said things. I could tell. That's *my* trick.'

'Useful too. Does that change anything for you?'

'No.'

'Pity.'

'Why?'

'I told you he went to see his sister. She's a pretty hopeless sort of case. Scared of everything. He certainly didn't give her any comfort.'

'He's not the sort of man who gives comfort, he gives energy and interest. Bit like you again.'

I coughed. 'Thanks.'

She got up off the couch and crossed to my chair. I could see her small breasts moving under the loose shirt and I wanted to touch them. She crouched in front of me.

'Touch.'

I touched. She took my hands away, lifted her shirt and spread my fingers and palms over her naked breasts. She was warm and when I bent down to kiss her she opened her mouth and locked on to me fiercely.

In bed she was enthusiastic and experienced. She slithered around, changing positions and exciting me with her small, hard body. She came in harsh, gasping spasms

106

and I was only a moment behind her. I propped up and looked down at her creamy oval face with the perfect cheekbones and brown smiling lips.

'Good?' she said.

'Yes.'

'Good.'

She squirmed out and pulled me down and went to sleep with her head on my shoulder. I went to sleep a little later when the sounds of the world that we'd blotted out started to filter back through to me. I knew that I'd been part of Erica Fong's revenge on William Mountain, but I didn't care.

15

SHE wasn't in the bed when I woke up. I put on my old towelling dressing gown and went downstairs towards the smell of brewing coffee. She was in the kitchen, fully dressed except for shoes and smoking her first fag of the day. She jumped when she saw me in the doorway; her slept-on hair was spiky here and matted flat there, like badly cut grass. She ran her hand over her head nervously.

'That was just . . . .'

'I know.' I went over and kissed the top of her head. I smoothed down some of the spiky hair. 'It's all right, Erica. Probably very good for both of us. No harm done.'

She put one arm around me, turned her head, inhaled and blew a stream of smoke away from me. 'Phew, thought it might be messy.'

'No. Let's have some coffee.'

Over the coffee I told her about my theory that Mountain was writing again.

'Madame didn't mention it.'

'Those little typewriters are silent, and you can fit one in an overnight bag.'

She nodded. 'Isn't that good, that he's writing?'

'The psychiatrist says it could go either way. I suppose it depends on what he's writing about.'

Her answering nod was glum, and we sat in silence for a while. I was conscious of a slight headache, maybe the result of sleeping on a stomach that was empty apart from some whisky. Toast and eggs suddenly appealed but I'd have been happier with a good idea.

'I can't imagine Bill not drinking,' Erica said. 'It'd be like

Max not barking. I can't imagine what he'd do with the time.'

I nodded. I could remember the first few heaving days of nicotine withdrawal and the desperate cravings of the few times I'd been alarmed by my alcohol consumption and had sworn off the stuff—life had seemed flat and the days full of dark, empty holes. I got up and put some stale bread in the toaster. Erica shook her head when I held up an egg.

'Bugger everything,' she said.

I started scrambling three eggs. 'How much ready money would he be likely to have?'

'Oh, tons. He made heaps from the TV writing and he didn't just do that one soapie. He did re-writes for other shows, script doctoring.'

'But he didn't get no satisfaction?'

She smiled. 'He said you patch shit up with more shit. He'd have plenty of cash and credit cards galore. I didn't find his cards in the house.'

'And nothing unusual apart from the notes?'

'Just one thing, a docket for a video camera, but no camera.'

The eggs were ready and the toast wasn't too black. I poured us both more coffee and sat down with the food. 'Maybe he went to New York to film Norman Mailer.'

She shook her head. 'No, he's here somewhere. 'Ome.'

'What?'

'That's what Madame told me—he said he was going 'ome.'

We arranged that she'd go home and feed Max and I'd have another shot at Mal. As a double act it wasn't much of a show but it was the best we could do. We went to the front door together, still talking. I reached past her and opened the door; she started to go through when the door suddenly swung in hard and threw her back at me. She dropped her bag and stumbled over it. I used both hands to catch her and my flabby friend from the car park stood in the doorway with a gun in his hand. The bitter-faced man stood beside him, and my brain, which had been too slow to anticipate exposing Erica to this sort of danger, worked fast enough to register that this must be Carl Peroni. He leered as Erica disentangled herself from me.

'Like to eat Chinese, do you, Hardy?' He laughed at his own joke, then he stepped back towards the gate and spoke in a respectful tone to someone in the street. 'It's okay. He's here and we're in.'

Flabby gestured with the gun which I noticed then was the Colt from my car, and Erica and I backed down the hallway. Peroni stood with his back to the wall to allow a small, thick-set man dressed in a dark, three-piece suit to pass him. He did so and moved past me on towards the back of the house as if he made forcible entries like this at least three times a day. His step was jaunty, and I stood in the hall and watched him check the kitchen and living room quickly before coming back and stepping neatly sideways through the first door off the hallway.

Flabby stood with his back to the front door and Peroni moved restlessly like a sheep dog yapping at heels, almost herding us into the front room. Erica stood close beside me; Peroni leaned against a wall and the small man in the suit stood in the middle of the room. He had an old-young face, unlined but jowly; his hair was white but thick, his eyes were deeply sunk but of a clear, untroubled blue.

'Mr Hardy, you can call me Mr Grey.' He had a light, prissy voice and speaking style with some traces of accent, possibly English.

'I can think of some other things to call you.'

'I daresay.' He looked at Peroni whose eyes were fixed on Erica. 'I want you to locate the telephone and unplug it. Then come back in here. Understand?'

Peroni nodded; he brushed past Erica, running his hand down her back, and went out. I'd already started to move towards him when Mr Grey took a small, flat gun from his pocket and pointed it at me.

'Don't!' he said.

I stopped. Erica got her cigarettes out of her pants pocket and put one in her mouth.

'Don't smoke, please,' Grey said. 'I suffer from sinus trouble.'

'Fuck your sinuses. I hope they flood.' She lit her cigarette and puffed.

Grey looked pained, then amused. 'Tough,' he said. 'All right, let's all be tough. I represent some people who want to locate William Mountain, a certain motor car and other items.'

Erica deliberately blew a cloud of smoke in his direction. 'We want to find him too.'

'Yes, now, searches have been made here, at Mountain's house and Miss Fong's flat.'

Erica coughed on her next draw. 'What about Max?'

Grey looked puzzled. He opened his jacket with his free hand and smoothed his vest over his light paunch. 'There was no-one there.'

'My dog.'

He smiled; he didn't like to be puzzled. 'Ah, yes, the dog was drugged, subdued. Nothing was found.'

I heard the fridge door open and close. *Maybe Peroni'll get drunk and cause a distraction*, I thought. Maybe he'll break a glass, cut himself and bleed to death. That'd only leave two men and two guns to contend with.

'What are you looking for?' I said.

Grey's smile faded. 'I believe you know that—a tape and a video film.'

'We haven't got them. Mountain must have them, and we don't know where he is.'

'Miss Fong?'

Erica shook her head.

'That's disappointing, very. You have a reputation for being persistent and resourceful in these matters, Mr

Hardy, and Miss Fong has spared no expense. I find it difficult to believe you. You have the advantage of knowing his friends and habits, Miss Fong. You have police contacts, Hardy. He is a semi-public man. I can't believe that you have come up with nothing.'

'You know what we know,' I said. 'I can't see what you hope to get out of this stuff with the guns and those clowns.'

Erica looked at me angrily. 'You both know more than I do. Who are these crims? What's this about tapes and videos?'

Grey buttoned his jacket again and sucked in some breath and stomach. He had an odd mannerism of stretching up, as if he'd been trying to make himself taller since he stopped growing at fourteen. 'Crims,' he said. 'Yes, as Miss Fong observes, they are crims. And you know crims can usually find each other. One or another can be made to talk or be bought. But Mountain is a different story; he has no criminal connections, none of any use anyway.'

I nodded, on the theory that he might be the sort of man who likes to be agreed with.

'Added to which,' he said slowly. 'I lack local knowledge. I do not live in this city.'

'That's your bad luck,' I said.

'I happen to think otherwise, but there we are. But I pride myself on being a good judge of character, Hardy. I believe you know things you won't reveal.'

'That's a professional manner I cultivate,' I said. 'Good for business.'

Grey frowned and moved the gun. Erica threw her cigarette butt at the fireplace and missed by a mile. 'He doesn't know anything. He doesn't!' She moved closer to me. 'He'd have told me. There's no point in killing him or beating him up.'

'Touching.' Grey sat down on the arm of a chair and flesh spread out on either side of his bottom. As I looked at him, taking in useless details like the ring with the big red stone in it that he wore on his left hand and his highly polished shoes, I suddenly realised that he was right. I *did* know something that I hadn't realised I knew until then. Another line of enquiry. I tried to blank the thought out in case Grey could read facial twitches and movements of the eyes. But he just pushed up with his polished shoes and levered his bum off the chair.

'I agree. No point in using force. Hardy's reputation for stubbornness exceeds that for intelligence. It wasn't an intelligent move to go to that coffee bar, was it, Hardy?'

I shook my head. 'Not as it turned out. Felt right at the time.'

'Besides, I'm a businessman and I don't think I could watch a man being tortured. And those two louts out there would probably make a mess of it.'

I tried to keep my voice steady. 'Probably.'

'*And*,' he emphasised the word with a slight movement of the gun, 'I don't want Hardy damaged because I want him to go on looking for Mountain.'

'He will,' Erica said.

'Exactly, but from now on he will be looking with a view to handing him over to me when he finds him.'

I saw it then and I didn't like it.

'He won't do that,' Erica said quickly. 'He's promised me he'll help Bill. We'll give the car back and try to keep Bill out of trouble.'

'Noble,' Grey purred, 'but it won't be like that.'

'Why not?' Erica snapped.

'Because we're going to take you away with us, my dear. And contrary to what I've just said, I'll give some thought to sending you back to Hardy in pieces in order to keep him keen. And if he finds Mountain he'll notify me or I'll kill you. You value Miss Fong's life more than Mountain's, don't you, Hardy?'

'Yes,' I said.

16

'No,' Erica said.

'Oh, yes. Hardy is being sensible; that's something else he's known for.'

'It sounds as if you've been doing some work on me.'

'Don't flatter yourself. It didn't take long and there wasn't anything subtle to find out.'

He wasn't trying to bait me, he was just stating the facts as he saw them. He was a man who dealt in facts. I was dealing with a few myself, trying to think of some way to head off this hostage strategy. This time Grey did seem to read my mind. He raised his voice while keeping the gun steady.

'Come on, you two. We're leaving!'

Flabby came into the room and gave me a look that suggested he hadn't forgiven me for the battering I gave him in the car park. Peroni strolled in with a glass of wine in his hand. He took a sip and then emptied the almost full glass on the carpet. The gesture marked him as the one who'd done over the house before. His face was creased in a smile showing his bad teeth and the fact that he enjoyed this sort of work. He tossed the wine glass in the fireplace where it broke. Erica jumped, and Peroni's grin widened until it changed into a wince of pain. He put his hand up to touch the puffiness around his jaw where it had slammed into the side of my car.

'You don't look so tough now,' he said.

'I was angry at the time.'

'Aren't you angry now?' He stepped up close and thrust his face forward so that I could smell his bad breath. He slapped me hard with his right hand; I rode back a bit, but the slap stung.

'I want a free go,' Flabby said.

I could feel blood from where my teeth had cut the inside of my mouth. 'I wouldn't if I were you,' I said. 'You're too slow. I could cripple you while you were shaping up.' I jerked my head at Grey. 'It's really the other way around—he needs me more than he needs you.'

'True,' Grey said crisply. 'Miss Fong is coming with us.' He went to the hallway door and gestured with his gun. We trooped into the hall and Grey looked at Erica's bag. 'Handy. We'll take that along. You can leave the liquor and cigarettes though. I'm a teetotaller myself.'

Erica looked desperately at me. I tried to look determined and resolute which is easier to do when you're not the one being carted away.

'Leave her the creature comforts, Grey. The smart hi-jackers keep the hostages happy.' I lifted the bag, zipped it up and handed it to Erica. 'Play along, love. He's more bark than bite. I'll do everything I can. How do I reach you, Grey?'

'You have an answering service?'

'Yes.'

'I'll leave messages, give you telephone numbers and instructions. You'd better take this seriously, Hardy.'

'I do. And you better understand that I'm not the only friend Miss Fong has in the world. There are some Chinese around who'll eat these two and you as well if anything happens to her. If you let Peroni touch her you can say goodbye to your balls and his.'

'I'll bear it in mind.' He nodded to Peroni who opened the door and they backed towards it so that I was facing two guns.

'Leave the Colt,' I said. 'I might need it.'

Flabby looked reluctant, but Grey's sharp nod made him set it down just inside the door.

'Your car is disabled, Hardy. Stay where you are for a minute or two and think. Do the work you're supposed to be so good at. There's no reason for your little friend to come to any harm.'

Erica's face was a mask of anger and fear; Peroni and Flabby went out and Grey followed, still keeping his little flat gun ready. He slammed the door. I stood in the hall and listened to car doors open and close. A well-tuned engine started and a car purred away.

I stood there for what seemed like hours but was probably only a few minutes. The cat came in and rubbed itself against my leg which meant that it wanted food. I opened the front door and looked at the Falcon parked across the road. It had no obvious list, so the disablement was probably mechanical. They'd closed the gate; Grey would probably have wiped his feet on the mat if I'd had one.

Under stress we revert to the old patterns. I re-plugged the phone and rang Grant Evans, gave him a description of Grey, and asked him to check it through as many computers as he could.

'He said he wasn't from Sydney,' I said.

'Lots of people aren't, you don't seem to grasp that. Getting sticky is it, Cliff?'

'It'll do.' I considered telling Grant about Erica and decided against it; if I needed a policeman on hand I had Frank Parker. Grant knew better than to pump me for more information.

'I'll get back to you if anything comes through. Anything else I can do?'

'Yeah. Keep a job as bottle washer open at the vineyard. I think that might be the kind of work I'm fit for.'

The idea that had come to me while Grey was accusing me of extra knowledge was simply that if Mountain was writing again, he might get in touch with his agent. It wasn't much of an idea but it was something. The other one or two writers I knew phoned their agents almost every day as if they expected them to wipe their noses and smooth life's stormy passage. Mountain seemed to make his own rules, but there was a chance he might conform in this way.

I phoned the Brent Carstairs Agency and at the mention of Mountain's name I was put through at wire-melting speed to a Mr Lambert.

'L'mb't here, y's?'

A New Zealander, hardly a vowel to his name. 'My name is Hardy, Mr Lambert. I'd like to talk to you about Bill Mountain. I'd say from the way they put me through to you that you'd be interested.'

'Most certainly, Mr Hardy. Where is he?'

'Hold on, why the interest? When I phoned a week ago some girl told me he was on holiday; she sounded as if she was just about on holiday herself. Why's everyone so keen now?'

'I'm afraid I can't discuss that,' he said sharply.

'You'd better discuss it. If you want to find him with all his typing fingers still attached, I'm your best bet.'

'I can't take that on faith. Who are you, exactly?'

'I'm a private detective, *exactly*. I also know Mountain slightly. I also know that he's writing again.'

Mr Lambert said: 'Mmm.' If you wanted caution he was your boy.

'I'll give you a sample. He's been to Marseilles and Nice recently, very recently. He's got inside a very dirty world that ninety-nine per cent of writers just read about in the papers. He's in danger. Do we talk?'

'Yes. Can you come to my office at once, please?'

The last literary agent I'd talked to had wanted me to follow his client day and night and report on her doings. He'd been careful not to touch anything I touched, and he had never once said please. The way Mr Lambert sounded, he might even say thank you.

The Falcon hadn't been disabled at all, another of the light, classy touches of Mr Grey, like returning my gun. I drove to Paddington through traffic that was light and good-tempered, unlike myself. I was feeling sour and under pressure—hostage-taking was one fashion I could do without. The agency was in one of those cute, twisting little thoroughfares off Oxford Street that are always one way in the direction you don't want. I worked my way to the right end and back up the street to park as close as I could. The street featured tall terraces with nose-in-the-air iron lace and fences with all the spear tops intact. There were offices that used to be houses and houses that used to be shops.

The agency office presented a lot of timber and lead-light glass to the street as if it was pretending to be an English pub. I pushed open the stripped and varnished timber door and walked into a carpeted space that was all soft lights and good taste. It looked more like an up-market bookshop than an office; the walls were lined with the best-sellers and instant remainders of Brent Carstairs clients. There was a rogues' gallery of writers' photographs with a heavy emphasis on those who had won awards and those whose works had made it to the large and small screens.

The only worker in sight was sitting at a desk in the deep bay window at the front of the place. She was wearing a severe grey suit, a white blouse and pearls. She lifted her head from the typescript she was reading and gave me a wintery smile.

'Yes?'

'Hardy,' I said, 'but not the writer. No plays, no poems, no novellas. I had an essay on shoe cleaning published in my school magazine, but that was a long time ago.'

'You're a humorist.'

'I wanted to see if I could make you smile.'

'You failed.'

'I'm a detective, here to see Mr Lambert. Smile at that.'

She didn't, but she did react. 'Oh, yes. About the Mountain manuscript; please go through there. Mr Lambert's waiting.'

She pointed a long, thin, grey arm at the apparently

blank wall at the end of the room but I didn't obey. I leaned close down to her, not expecting any perfume and not getting any. 'Manuscript?' I said.

'Oh, God, I'm talking out of turn. Please see Mr Lambert. He'll explain everything.'

I straightened up and peered at the wall. 'I've been waiting all my life for someone who could explain everything.'

'Please!'

Two pleases was urgent stuff from the likes of her; I followed her stabbing finger, and after walking across a few thousand dollars' worth of carpet paid for by the authors whose books I passed, I found a door discreetly hidden in the wall. I knocked and Lambert called out: 'Come in!' as if I was David Williamson come to sign up for life. He was half way across his office towards the door by the time I got it open. His hand came out so fast I nearly ducked and countered.

'Mr Hardy, come in, come in.' We shook hands and he practically donated his to me. He stuck his head through the open door and asked the woman behind the desk to bring us some coffee. Lambert's office was a smaller version of the other room: bearded faces gazed out from dust jackets, review headlines announced biting wit and experimental irony.

Lambert was a medium-sized man with a thick waist and lank hair that was greying and thinning as if there was a race on to make him either white or bald. He didn't help matters by wearing a spotted bow tie and a patterned vest that had food and drink stains on it. He ushered me into a chair, scooted behind his desk and plopped his glasses down in front of him. The lenses were heavily smudged.

'Your phone call intrigued me, Mr Hardy, I must say.'

'So I see. What's the name of the woman outside?'

'Maud.'

'I'd never have guessed that. She's very jumpy, and so are you.'

To prove he wasn't jumpy he picked up his glasses and put them on. Then he took them off again. Before he could demonstrate any more sang froid. Maud came in with a silver tray on which sat china cups and bowls and a big pot of coffee. As she was pouring, I recalled that I'd had mainly whisky for dinner and no breakfast.

'Would you have a biscuit or anything about?' I said. 'I haven't eaten in quite a while.' I took a thirsty slurp of the coffee. It always impresses people to tell them you haven't eaten; it makes you look busier than them. Lambert reacted as if he would've sent out for steak and eggs.

'I'm quite sure we'd have something. Could you see to it, Maud?'

Maud said she would, and I drained my cup and poured another, adding sugar and stirring. Lambert sipped his and waited. He used a napkin to wipe his glasses and only succeeded in spreading the goo around. Maud trotted back in with a plate of ginger nuts and I had two dipped and up to the mouth before she reached the door.

I got the biscuits down before I started talking. 'Bill Mountain's writing again; he's sent you something that's got you all excited—a novel?'

He nodded, then he shook his head. 'A synopsis,' he breathed, 'an absolutely brilliant outline of a sure-fire best seller. Amazing!'

I reached across the desk for the pot and Lambert took his bum off the seat to push it towards me; he'd have given me the pot and the tray if I'd asked for them.

'You seem surprised that he could write a book,' I said.

Lambert sipped his milky coffee and spilled some biscuit crumbs down his vest. 'I thought he was washed up except for TV writing, and he seemed to be losing his grip on that—missing deadlines, messing around with the characters. He's a terrible drinker.'

'Was,' I said. 'He's stopped.'

'I know.'

'How d'you know? I found out from his sister in

Melbourne a couple of days ago. The news couldn't be all over Sydney yet.'

He looked at me, and suddenly jerked his head half around. I realised that he'd done it before; it was a nervous mannerism, but it made it look as if he was afraid someone was going to grab him and send him back to New Zealand. He didn't look particularly smart, but he was good at keeping his mouth shut. Another swallow of coffee and the penny dropped.

'I get it. He talks about drying-out in the synopsis. The book's autobiographical.'

He nodded.

'Jesus, does a man get killed up in the mountains? Does the hero buy smack in Marseilles?'

More nods.

'This is important, Mr Lambert. If you have any way of contacting him you must tell me. His life's in danger.' Nothing changed in Lambert's expression and I realised that it was like telling someone about a film they'd already seen. 'You know that.'

He put some more fingerprints on the lenses of his glasses. 'The protagonist speculates about the retribution that awaits him—compelling stuff.'

'How does it end?'

He lay back in his chair. His head tilted and I could see the dark bags of sleep debt under his eyes. He pulled at the silly bow tie and it came undone untidily down the front of his shirt.

'Wouldn't have a cigarette, would you?' he said.

'I gave it up.'

'So did I, years ago when I first came here. I was so glad to be here, I felt I could do without them and I did, until now. I don't know how it ends—the synopsis doesn't end. He runs the story on to about . . . I'm guessing here, five chapters from the end? It's a masterly piece of work . . . I've read thousands . . . I could get a quarter of a million advance from a top publisher, maybe more.'

Apparently I was expected to be impressed by the sum of money. I was. I gave the sort of nod you give to a quarter of a million bucks.

'All right, Mr Hardy, I've put you in the picture. What's your interest?'

'I was hired by the owner of the used car firm.'

It was as if we were speaking in a code, mutually mastered. 'I see.'

'I've met some people connected with the organisation behind the car thefts.'

'Rough?'

'Pretty rough. The honours are all their way at the moment.' I realised that I couldn't tell Lambert too much, couldn't tell him, for example, that I'd sell his writer in a flash to get Erica back.

'Mountain describes them as killers; is he exaggerating?'

I thought about it. 'Does he describe himself as a killer?'

'The protagonist kills a man in self-defence.'

'Uh huh, well, I don't know of anyone they've killed. There're two men in a bad way in hospital who offended them, and they'd have done the same or worse to me if it had turned out that way. They certainly intend to kill Mountain.' I threw that in to keep Lambert on his toes—I assumed that a synopsis is worthless. I knew that dead men don't write novels.

'If you think you can prevent that I'll be happy to co-operate in any way. Funds are not a problem.'

'I'm trying. Why haven't you gone to the police?'

'The outline came in the post with a note in which Mountain said he would cease to be my client if I called the police into the matter at any point. Literary agents have no contracts with their clients, you know. It's a gentleman's arrangement, cancellable by either party, at any time.'

'That right? Sounds a bit like my work. You're on ten per cent, are you?'

'Dearly earned, believe me.'

'Okay. Well, I'll have to see the note and the outline, of course, and I'll take some more coffee if you've got it.'

He jerked his head over his shoulder and fiddled with his glasses.

'No more coffee?'

'Of course there's more coffee. It's letting you see the synopsis . . . .'

'Anything to help—your very words.'

'I don't want it shown about. A lot of the impact would depend on the novelty, the element of surprise . . . .'

'You're beginning to worry me, Mr Lambert. I wouldn't send the thing to Random House. All I want is to find Mountain; I have to see what he's written. That's flat!'

'I don't know.'

He looked so perturbed that I had to soften the blow a little. Would you like me to say that we've got a gentleman's agreement that I'll keep the thing totally confidential?'

'That would help.'

He nodded. I stacked the cups on the tray, picked it up and went to the door. Maud had put a chair within earshot of the door and was doing some filing with the antennae fully extended. She started when I opened the door.

'It's okay,' I said. 'Everybody's interested. Could you let us have some more coffee, please?'

She took the tray and headed towards wherever they kept the Andronicus. Lambert had got up from his desk and was turning a key in a filing cabinet lock. He pulled out a drawer, extracted a manila folder and slid it across the desk towards me, I'd expected him to make more of a ritual of it. I opened the folder and found a stack of A4 size photocopy sheets. I closed the cover.

'This is a photocopy, I want to see the original.'

'Why?'

I leaned forward and whispered. 'Because there might be something written on the backs of the sheets.'

'I didn't think of that.' Back to the filing cabinet, out with the key, twiddle, twiddle, scrape and another folder appeared. The typeface was the same as on Erica's card and there were probably signs of the same 'fist' and the identical displacement of the 'e' if you cared for those sorts of things. I looked at the backs of the sheets, but there was nothing on them. I hadn't expected anything, but you never know. Lambert had stood, hovering, with his hands out, and I gave the folder back.

'Thanks. I'd like to see the note, too.'

Maud came in with the coffee and I smiled at her. She looked at me in awe and I realised that it was because I was holding a copy of *it* in my hands. I smiled at her and she smiled back. All I needed was something worth a quarter of a million and she was a pushover.

Lambert watched her walk out and passed me the note. It was brief and simple; I asked Lambert for a copy of it and he dug one out. We both swilled down a cup of coffee. I tapped the edges of the paper straight in the folder and got up.

Lambert looked alarmed. 'Ah,' he said. The head flicked left.

'Yes?'

'Aren't you going to read it now? It's not long. Tell me what you think ...?'

'Haven't you read any books? I need a blonde, a bottle and a dark room.'

He shook his head and sighed.

'Don't worry, Mr Lambert, look on the bright side.' I moved to the door.

'And what's that?'

'You've got other clients.'

I heard his groan through the closed door.

17

I⸀T was hard work appearing confident to Lambert. If he'd known how desperate things really were, he'd probably have risked Mountain's ire by calling in the cops; and if he really knew his business, he could have made a deal with any other agent Mountain might defect to. That sort of thinking made me wonder what Mountain would do if he knew Erica was a hostage—maybe he'd do nothing, maybe he'd just write about it, adjusting his program whatever that was, or maybe it would send him crazier than he was already. Mere speculation. I had no way of telling him about it, and if he was close enough to the action to know I'd be running into him soon.

On the drive back to Glebe, with the folder on the seat beside me, I realised that I hadn't asked Lambert about the delivery or posting of the outline. There might have been something to learn from postmarks or dates. Probably not, but I clearly wasn't at the top of my form. I had the bad feeling of being manipulated by events, and a worse one of being flat out of ideas.

I had had the sense to look for a tail on the drive to Paddington in case Grey thought I was about to do something decisive and I checked again on the way back. No tail. I didn't like the idea of Grey spooking Lambert into handing over the synopsis, and it would have been a pity to let Peroni get to work on the bone china.

The cat was out, the letter box was empty, there were no dishes to wash—there was no excuse for delaying an inspection of Bill Mountain's opus, or outline of opus. I made myself a sandwich and took it, the folder and a flagon of wine out into the imitation of a backyard. Hilde had introduced some plants and done something with bricks and planks of wood, which meant that there was somewhere to sit out there other than on the toilet which had been my pre-Hilde perch. A couple of the plants looked sick as if they missed Hilde too. The afternoon sun was warm; I took off my shirt, poured some wine and got to work.

The note was unremarkable; Mountain was a neat, accurate typist:

> *Dear Keith,*
>
> *This synopsis will give you a cockstand. The first draft is well underway; I'm not drinking and I'm writing thousands of words a day. Read it, talk to publishers, but don't show it to anyone. Put together the best deal you can. Say one word to the police and this is all you'll ever see of it. Ten per cent of zero is zero. Do it the way I say. I'll be in touch.*
>
> *yrs.*

The signature was a scrawled 'B'. I drank some wine, ate some sandwich and began to read the typescript.

I'm not the fastest reader in the world, and synopses are not the easiest things to read. I'd had to plough through a lot of them in my brief career as a law student and I never found them much fun. It took me an hour and several glasses of wine to work through Mountain's forty pages. When I'd finished I was sitting in shadow and should have been cold, but I didn't notice. The book was a knock-out.

Here and there Mountain had inserted short passages of dialogue and descriptive bits among the bare bones of the story. To my jaded and untutored eye the writing seemed crisp and dramatic but unobtrusive. It wouldn't hold up the action, and there was plenty of that. The protagonist, as Lambert had called him, was a thinly-disguised version

126

of Mountain himself, except that he was a film-writer, not a TV hack. More marketable, see, right off the bat. His name was Morgan Shaw. This writer gets drawn into the car-stealing business more thoroughly than he wanted. Initially, he was just doing some research for a script. Shaw writes the movie in scene break-down form as he lives it—including the taping of the instructions and the filming of the car pick-up. He gets addicted to the danger and baits his employers by leaving a taped message himself in the locker at Central Railway, where he picks up the papers that secure him the Audi.

In Mountain's book there was to be a long chapter on the killing at Blackheath where Morgan Shaw had gone to indulge his two great weaknesses—women and booze. The killing was in some way cathartic.

All this, except the catharsis, was pretty familiar territory, but a new element entered the story—a journalist whom Shaw contacts to get information about heroin in Sydney. This character, given the name of Andrew Hope by Mountain, is full bottle on the subject, and the source of technical detail on the opium poppy, processing and marketing, as well as local colour. à la Forsythe and Elegant. The travel to Marseilles, Nice and along the Riviera would be there as a strong selling point, and a harrowing 'lost weekend' section where the writer kicks the booze.

I found myself reading and re-reading passages with interest and enjoyment. Mountain had made Morgan Shaw a more attractive character than himself, wittier and more compassionate. Ruthless and capable too, but the Mountain I knew and disliked seemed to be scoring pretty high on those counts. The sample scenes from the movie included in the outline were dramatic and direct, and held the thing together. Another selling point—it was half way to being a movie already.

The most alarming thing was that the manuscript ended with Shaw back in Sydney with a large supply of pure

127

heroin and cocaine and some useful contacts. He has a plan to establish a drug empire and use the profits to fund pornographic films, rock bands and counter-culture communes. But the writer himself becomes addicted to heroin very quickly, and the signs were of a disintegration of some kind being held together by fantasy.

The last scene broached a new subject:

> *'He looked at the heroin for a long time. There was enough for him to make his exit through a tunnel of warm pleasure. He'd have time to sit in a padded chair and say a long, sweet goodbye and wait for the flash that would mean the doors to the tunnel were opening.'*

The warm pleasure was being imparted by various women whom Mountain must have conjured up partly from his imagination and partly, if Erica had it right, from memory. At the point where the outline broke off, our Morgan had a lot of irons in the fire; he was plotting the set-up of his network, still baiting the car thieves with copies of false documents and real tapes, and playing around with the idea of suicide. Lambert, reading the stuff as autobiographical, must have been able to hear his knees knock. His ten per cent couldn't have seemed very safe.

I flicked through the pages looking for clues, slips, conscious or unconscious signposts to where Mountain might be. No luck. Place names were potent and well-chosen, but fictitious. The typewriter he was using had a correcting function, so that if he had had second thoughts about identifying places too closely and made changes there was no record of it in the typescript. It was like reading a deposition by someone who had sworn to tell the truth but had no inhibitions about committing perjury. On the last page, Shaw was in a hotel not far from the heart of a major city, which could mean that Mountain was in a private house somewhere in the backblocks.

I made a list of the apparently important things in the manuscript, and checked it against other information I had. Nothing happened; there were confirmations of the obvious things like the alcohol cure and the heroin purchase, but nothing on the movements or locations or the suicide idea. Small comfort in that. Next I listed the characters, and entered the few remarks and descriptions allotted them in the synopsis. This amounted to little more than a thumbnail sketch in most cases, but provided more confirmation. Mal was recognisably there as 'Eddie', the writer's first contact with the criminal world; poor Miss Mountain was there, her fragile, suburban respectability brutally etched. Other characters were either heavily disguised or fictitious but the portrait of the journalist, Andrew Hope, rang some bells. My notes on him read: *Andrew Hope, 35, dark, heavy build, journalist, ex-football player, practical joker, gambler, experimental drug user.*

Arthur Henderson was fifty-two, not thirty-five: he was short and fair and had been a good tennis player. But he was a freelance journalist, said to be the first man to take cocaine on television (accounts differ on whether the substance he had sniffed on The Jimmie Martin Show really *was* cocaine), and his idea of a joke was to balance a bucket of piss over a door and sit back to watch the result.

I'd had some dealings with Henderson, but I didn't have a way of contacting him. As it turned out, doing this was like trying to read the label on a turning record—you can almost do it but not quite. The first few calls I made got me nowhere except from one blank wall to another. There was no other course open than to add another favour to the long list I already owed Harry Tickener. Since Harry became deputy editor of *The News* rather than its star reporter, he sees and hears less than he used to, but still more than most. He took my call, but I had the feeling that he had at least one other phone to his ear.

'Hi, Cliff, I'm busy. How're you?'

'Trying to be busy, Harry. When did you last see Arthur Henderson?'

'Who?'

'Artie Henderson—when did you last see him?'

'I can't answer that.'

'Why not? I thought he hounded your place to flog his stuff. It can't be that long.'

Harry laughed and gave one of his forty-Camels-a-day dry coughs. 'I'm joking, Cliff. It's like Philosophy. You ever do Philosophy?'

'No, Harry.'

'You don't know that thing about stepping into the same river twice?'

'No, sounds like a dumb thing to do.'

'Yeah, well. I can't answer the question "when did I last see Arthur Henderson" because I'm looking at him right now. He's here trying to interest the editor in a piece on Tim Tully. Ever heard of Tully?'

'No.'

'Nor has the editor. What . . . .'

'Harry, hold onto him. I've got to see him. Buy him a drink.'

'That's asking too much, Cliff. I've never heard of Tully either, and I don't want to.'

'Do anything you like to him, but don't let him get away.'

'Is it life or death or money?'

'All of them.'

Harry laughed and coughed again. 'Okay, Cliff. He'll be here, but hurry.'

I slammed down the phone and rushed out of the house, still buttoning my shirt. There was a white envelope lying on the doorstep; I swooped on it and crammed it into my shirt pocket as I felt for my keys. It wasn't until I stopped at some lights that I could open the envelope. It had my name printed in block capitals on the front and inside was a thick clump of straight, black, Oriental hair.

18

THE reporters' room at *The News* was busy as usual
with men and women whaling away at computer
keyboards, telephones ringing and filing cabinet drawers
shrieking. I couldn't see Arthur Henderson when I walked
in, but Harry Tickener was there. He seemed to have
shrunk over recent years, but perhaps it's just that his
desks had got bigger. The surface of the one he was at
now was covered with telephones, writing pads, print-out
paper and a couple of gross of pens and pencils. Harry had
kept up the journo's tradition of an up-ended typewriter
on his desk, although it's doubtful that he had much use
for it anymore. He also used to have a use for the
pencils—to scratch at his hair—but there wasn't enough
hair left now to scratch.

He saw me coming from across the room and made a
show of grabbing up some paper and running. He stood
his ground though, and lit one of his Camels. When I got
close enough he blew smoke in my face.

'Any regrets?'

I waved the smoke away. 'None. I pull my lungs out
from time to time to have a look at them. You'd need a
fishnet to get yours up.' I stabbed at his thin chest. 'With a
fine mesh!'

'Charming. You're probably right, but my old man's
smoked fifty a day for nearly sixty years, and there isn't a
hill in North Sydney he can't walk up. I'm a great believer
in heredity. I suppose you want to know where Artie is?'

'Right.'

'I'm sorry; we couldn't keep him. The stuff he had was
so bad there was nothing to say. But we did you a favour.

He's so depressed he'd have headed for the pub.'

'Shit, Harry, there's a lot of pubs in Sydney.'

'Artie's a lazy bugger, he'll have taken the Continental across the road, nothing surer.' He was back behind his desk before he finished talking; it's hard to hold Harry's attention these days unless you've got a leaked document or a film of the politician actually taking the money. He took a paper out from under an identical stack of other papers; the total chaos of his desk is an orderly filing system in Harry's mind. He glanced up at me dismissively.

'Must have a drink sometime, Cliff. Or have you given that up too?'

'No, Harry. I haven't given it up. I'm humbled by your help and I'd like to have a drink with you. Give me a ring when you get a quarter hour off.'

He grinned, drew defiantly on the cigarette and bent his pale pink skull over his papers.

The Continental is a typical journalists' pub with different bars suited to different purposes. There's one for talking or reading the papers in peace, one for eating after a fashion and another for fighting. Artie Henderson was in the fighting bar. I hoped Harry hadn't mentioned to him that I wanted to see him, because one of Henderson's chief characteristcs is suspicion. He is suspicious of everybody and everything. Most of his published articles in recent years had been paranoid conspiracy pieces with just enough substance in them to get a run after heavy editing.

He saw me, and he had money on the counter and was heading for the door, preparing to skirt around me, before I was one step into the bar. I blocked him.

'Artie, I'd like a word.'

He tried to step around me, but he'd had a bit too much already and his reflexes were shot; I side-stepped faster and baulked him off balance. He stumbled and lurched towards the nearest table for support. The few other drinkers didn't even look around; it'd take six good punches and some blood to get them interested. Artie breathed hard and pushed up from the table but I pushed him down again. He was badly out of condition and went down easier and harder than I'd expected. I helped him up onto a stool near one of the pillars that divided the room. He leaned back against the pillar, and his hand searched automatically on the shelf nearby for his drink. He was in a bad way.

'Take it easy, Artie,' I said. 'Just stay right there and I'll get you a drink.'

He nodded resignedly, but I kept my eye on him as I backed off to the bar. He lit a cigarette, coughed cataclysmically and wheezed, but he stayed where he was. When I got back with a scotch for him and some red wine for me, he was breathing better and his eyes were bright with anticipation, maybe for the whisky, maybe for calamity. He put the scotch down in one gulp, sucked on his cigarette and rubbed his back where it had hit the wall.

'I don't want to talk to you, Hardy. You're trouble in large doses. Jeez, me back hurts . . . .'

'Don't be like that, Artie. I just reacted automatically to your side-step. You've slowed down.'

He sighed. 'At everything; at some things I've bloody stopped. All right, Hardy, get us another drink and let's hear what's on your excuse for a mind.'

I put five dollars down by his empty glass and his pudgy, liver-spotted hand reached for it automatically.

'You buy the drinks, Artie. The walk'll do you good.'

He heaved his bulky body off the stool and shuffled across to the bar. His suit bagged at all pockets with the weight of assorted articles, and his shoes hadn't been cleaned that year. If he'd had any contact with Bill Mountain recently, it hadn't done him any financial good unless he'd already drunk it. He came back with a double scotch and beer chaser and a packet of cigarettes, all bought from my five. He put the couple of coins in change down on the shelf and gave me one of his rare smiles.

'There you are, Cliff. Shocking price things are today.'

I lifted what was left in my glass. 'Cheers, Artie. Quick trip to the grave.'

'You always were a humorist, Cliff. What's up?'

'When did you last see Bill Mountain?'

He sipped his whisky and tapped the side of his head where his pepper-and-salt hair stood up untidily over his ears. 'Dreadful memory,' he said. '*Have* I seen old Bill lately?'

'Yeah. You'll be flattered to hear he's been writing about you.'

'Me?' He looked as alarmed as if he'd discovered that his fly was open.

'You. This is a secret, but I'm telling you because I can't see how you'd make any money out of it. Mountain's writing a novel. He's got a character in it who's unmistakably you. Like Fleming and Le Carré used Dicky Hughes, you know?'

He nodded, I assume flattered.

'Well, this character gives the hero the drum on the heroin racket.'

Artie's eyes narrowed in a parody of cunning. 'We did have a word or two on the subject.'

'Right. I suppose he told you he was researching for a TV script?'

'Exactly.' The scotch was nearly all gone and he started on the beer.

'But he's gone and got himself personally involved in the business.'

'Jesus!'

'The less you know the better, but what I want you to do is tell me everything you told him—the names, the places, the procedures. Anything that might help me get a line on him. He's history unless someone pulls him out of it. I don't have to tell you that.'

'Sure. I assume someone's employing you, Cliff?'

'Yeah, I'm not poking into this for fun, believe me. I assume it's all going on around Darlo and Bondi and I know there used to be a nice phone hook-up between the Customs and a city hotel we won't mention. But I'm a bit out of touch. Put me in touch, Artie.'

I didn't recognise the sound at first; it came from deep within his frowsy frame, and he shook like a man hanging onto a pneumatic drill. It ended in a shuddering spasm and a series of coughs that started at his ankles. His face flushed red and his hand shook violently when he picked up his glass. He got a swallow down and resumed normal breathing. It was Artie's way of laughing; if he did it too often he'd drop dead. 'That's rich, Cliff, really rich. Darlo! Phone hook-up! You think it's all kids and hard cases, eh? Out of touch? You don't even know what the bloody game is.' His wide grin threatened to split into spasm again. I gripped his upper arm and dug my fingers into the spongy flesh until I felt him tense up in the pain.

'Cut out the bullshit, Artie. You've had your laugh. Okay, I've got it all wrong—steer me straight.'

'Anything in it for me?'

'If I get a result, maybe.'

'Hardly a promise, but I'll trust you. I've got bloody little coming in. Okay, Mountain knew more about it than you, but not enough. All that sleazy stuff still goes on, always has, always will. I've written a bit about it . . . .'

'I don't want your CV, Artie. Get on with it.'

'There's a whole new drug market opened up. Lots of professional people are skin popping, sniffing, smoking— all that. Some are weekend users and they stay that way. You'd be surprised at some of the jobs they hold down. Top people or on their way to the top. Young and youngish is what I'm talking about, but there's some oldies too. They don't just go down the usual places to score, d'you follow?'

I nodded. 'So what do they do?'

'It's a sociological thing, really. The people with the money write the rules ...'

'Save it, Artie. What happens?'

'They do it the way they do everything, old son. They hold parties.'

'Parties?'

'Exactly. Lots of 'em. There's a circuit, or a couple of circuits. Certain people get invited, and they bring along certain substances. These people don't keep a stash, see? They don't want to think about it during the week while they're being managing this and executive that. Quality people with quality money for quality stuff.'

'This is what Mountain wanted to hear about?'

'Yep. Another drink?'

He was asking, not offering. I did want another drink and I got up to get it automatically, with my mind mostly on the scene Artie had sketched. I was half way to the bar when Artie made a bolt for it; he would have made it but Harry Tickener chose that moment to open the inward swinging door and Artie had to step back. By that time I had my hand on his shoulder again. Harry looked surprised.

'Just off? Thought I'd join you.'

'Where's your desk, didn't you bring it?' I got a firm grip on Artie's shoulder pad and turned him around. 'Good to see you, Harry. Let's all have a drink. Artie here just got the wrong door. He was looking for the bog.'

'I need it, too.' Artie growled. 'Get a round, Hardy. I'll be back in a minute.' He shuffled off unsteadily towards the door on which some wag had altered the word to read 'Bents'. Tickener and I sat down near the pillar.

'Can he get out of the dunny?'

Harry raised an eyebrow to near where his hairline used to be. 'Like that is it? No, I don't think so. I think the loo's down below street level.'

I got some more scotch for Henderson, the same for Harry and wine for me. I filled Harry in quickly on what

Artie had told me, but I didn't say why I'd been pumping. Harry lit a Camel and dragged on it hard.

'We ran a story on that stuff a while ago,' he said. 'You must have missed it.'

'I was probably in the middle of *The Brothers Karamazov*. Artie seems to be full bottle; would he have some names d'you reckon?'

'Bound to.'

Artie came back with damp hands. He grabbed his glass and swore as it almost slipped through his fingers. But he got half of the whisky down and finished his beer. 'That wasn't a bad piece, Harry,' he whined. 'You should've put in a word . . . .'

'Skip it!' I said, 'Let's hear a bit more about the yuppies and drugs.'

'I told you. Parties. Everybody's got a legitimate invitation. Hosts do the buying. Take it in turns. All kosher.'

Harry nodded. Artie nicked a Camel from Harry's pack. 'I don't know,' I said. 'Sounds like kid stuff.'

Artie shrugged; he would have been willing to let it stand there, but Harry wasn't. If it had been printed in *The News*, Harry Tickener was there to defend it. 'Don't you believe it,' he said. 'These people call themselves recreational drug users; they say they've got it all under control, but they haven't, not all of them. Some of them get properly hooked like any dumb kid on the dole, and they need a supply just as badly. They've got the money— at least to start with. You know that, Artie.'

'Sure.' Harry had touched Artie's professional pride as he'd intended. 'That's right, the hooked ones have to deal bigger to keep a supply, just like Harry says. Gets to be a pressure game. Harry, would you like a piece . . . .'

'No. But you can help Cliff a bit more than that, can't you, Artie?'

'What's in it for me?'

'No double dipping, Artie,' I said. 'You'll be seen to if I get somewhere.'

Artie could wheedle with the best of them. 'I could do a piece on that council, Harry. I know who's on the take from who.'

'Whom,' Harry said. 'Maybe.'

'Well, there's a bit of a party circuit up on the North Shore, Pymble way.'

'Names,' I said.

'I've only got two: Gamble—that's Anthony Gamble on Lady Jane Drive. And a woman named Deirdre Kelly—Montague Street, I think.'

Harry went off to the toilet, and I wrote the names down. 'Are they recreational or hooked?'

Henderson shrugged. He looked weary, as if the effort of parting with information without immediate financial return had drained him of energy. 'I heard they were on the way to being hooked. The number of gatherings has gone up or something. That's the sign, see? You didn't get this from me, of course.'

'Naturally not. This what you told Mountain?'

He nodded.

'Haven't seen him since?'

'Not hide nor hair of him.'

'If you do, you could ask him to get in touch with me.'

He got down off his stool and hitched up his sagging trousers, fighting for a bit of dignity as Harry rejoined us. 'I might do that, Cliff. See you, Harry.' He walked away swaying a little and pausing at the open door to make sure he had the all-clear. Harry watched him go, and shook his head.

'Sad case.'

'Would that article you ran on this stuff be worth reading?'

'You can hurt, Cliff, you can really wound. Buy me another drink and I'll dig it out so you can see for yourself. How's Helen?'

'She's up the bush,' I said, 'worse luck.'

19

I sat in the library next to the reporters' room at *The News*, and read the article about the professional persons who used drugs recreationally. In a way, it was like reading Bill Mountain's synopsis; the people interviewed talked freely and articulately, but they had been given false names, and it was hard to tell whether they were lying. None admitted to being hooked, and none would give any information out on how they obtained the drugs. The drugs, doses, effects and justifications for what they were doing, they would talk about *ad nauseam*.

The reporter presented the material straight and with an oddly incurious air, as if he had found his informants rather boring. Hard facts were few—the North Shore was one of the centres of the activity and the participants feared only two things—exposure as drug-users to their straight professional colleagues, and accidental overdose.

I called on Harry after I'd read the article. I knew the protocol now.

'Great piece,' I said. 'Your idea?'

'Partly.'

'Any reaction to it?'

'A lot. Plenty of denials, advice from doctors about the perils of addiction, worried letters from employers who suspected their staff and from staff who suspected other staff. Lots of defensiveness and paranoia.'

'Police response?'

'Complete silence. Before you ask, Cliff, I checked the files on the two people Artie named. Nothing on Gamble, minor item on the woman. She was attacked outside her flat a few months ago and got cut up a bit. Claimed to have no idea of the reason.'

'Thanks, Harry. With all this information at your disposal, why don't you write a novel? They say there's big dough in it if you get it right.'

Tickener rubbed the smooth shiny skin on the top of his head. 'Fuck you, Cliff. I've written six, can't get 'em published. Now that you've thoroughly depressed me, you can piss off.'

I went, leaving him to rub his shiny head. Maybe if he rubbed it the right way it'd conjure up a genie who'd help him get his novels published.

An instinct told me that this was something like the right track. Dealing with the young, upwardly-mobile drug-interested sounded just like Mountain's style, and the subject seemed like a good fresh one for popular fiction. One article in *The News* was hardly over-exposure.

It was late in the afternoon, with heavy traffic building. The weather had turned uncertain; the sky was a leaden grey, purplish in the distance, and the wind was an irritable, swirling thing that seemed to be snapping at the nerves of the people in the street. More than usually, they were jay-walking, misjudging speeds and mouthing obscenities at the drivers, me included.

Part of Elizabeth Street was being torn up and, with the number of lanes reduced, the cars moved along in snarling, resentful jerks. It took me almost an hour to get from Broadway up to St Peter's Lane, and I had an aching head and a dry throat when I got there. An hour of swearing and being sworn at is bad preparation for anything; the stairs up to the floor where my office is seemed to have doubled and got steeper, and the corridor looked longer and gloomier than usual.

I opened the door, and the letters inside skittered across the floor. I left them there and ran the answering machine tape. The first two calls signified nothing; the third was crisp and to the point:

'Hardy,' the voice was light, neutral-sounding—possibly Grey's. 'Message: call 827 3410 before midnight without fail. Whether you have anything to say or not.'

I wanted to talk back to the voice, ask it to be reasonable, enter into dialogue, maybe work out a deal. But the message was as brief and uncommunicative as a classified ad. Grey had a sound psychogical grasp though. After another business message the voice came through again:

'The girl is in good health.'

Unless Hardy screws up. I thought. I ran the rest of the tape in hope that there might be some good news on it. The last message was a somewhat breathless one from Lambert, the literary facilitator, asking me to call him urgently. I got Maud first, but she put me through without any chat. When Lambert answered, I imagined I could see him twisting his head in that nervous, persecuted manner. I felt like doing some head-twisting myself.

'Oh, God! Thanks for calling, Hardy. Another section of the synopsis has just arrived.'

I thought I'd ask the sleuthly question first this time. 'How was it delivered?'

'What? Oh, by mail. Special delivery or something.'

'Posted in Sydney?'

'How do I know? Oh, I see, the envelope. I'll get Maud to look. Does it really matter?'

'Don't know,' I grunted. 'Well, what does he say?'

He wasn't a complete fool, and he remembered that he was getting my time for free. 'What have you come up with?'

'Some things, some names. I could be getting closer. But what he's writing is still crucial. I need to know.'

'Of course. Well, it's frightful, gripping stuff . . . but very disturbing.'

'Can you still hear the cash registers?'

'I'll ignore that. I'd be a hypocrite if I said it wasn't

commercial; but the disturbing thing is that the suicide motif seems to be getting stronger. The hero . . .' he broke off and coughed, 'well, the protagonist is well and truly hooked on the drugs he's selling, and he's developed a new interest.'

'Hold on, I'm more interested in threats. He's still being threatened by the original crims, the car people?'

'Umm, he feels so, and also by people involved in the drug business. He's stepping on toes there, but there's something worse.'

'Jesus, worse?'

'It's another level of threat, really, and coming from himself. He's sort of splitting into two personalities and the one threatens the other with physical extinction.' I could hear the excitement in his voice; maybe the breathlessness had come from ringing me while reading the last few words. 'It's extraordinary. I've never read anything like it—very contemporary and powerful.'

'You're writing the reviews, Mr Lambert. I wouldn't if I were you. Any note with it?'

'No.'

'I'm going to need to see this. Can you run me off a copy? I'll come by and get it now.'

'I can do that, yes. Do you really think you're getting somewhere?'

Oddly, I thought I was. I had a feeling that I was gaining on William Mountain, but I also had a feeling that he knew he was being gained on. I made encouraging noises to Lambert, and left the office. On the stairs I remembered that I hadn't made a note of the contact number Grey, if it was Grey, had left. I swore, and went back and wrote it down. On the stairs again and I realised that I hadn't looked at the mail; this time I just swore and kept going.

Maud was waiting for me just inside the door at Brent Carstairs. She handed me a manila envelope, ritually, as if it contained the Bruce-Partington plans, and waited for me to make a smart remark. I fooled her.

Lambert evidently didn't want to see me, and I could live with that. I wanted to think of the synopsis as cards in my hand and Erica's safety as the pot. I didn't want to see Lambert's bow tie or the best-seller-at-risk look in his eyes.

When I got back to Glebe, Hilde was there collecting some pot plants from the garden and some other things she'd left behind in the house. She was about four months pregnant, very happy, and had never looked better. She kissed me and stood back.

'You look like hell, Cliff. What've you been doing to yourself?'

I tried to review my day—Grey, Tickener, Henderson, Lambert: unloving company—no wonder I wasn't looking my freshest. I grunted something unintelligible, and peered through the dusty window at the backyard, which looked a bit more dusty itself now that a couple of the pots had gone. Hilde pulled at the envelope in my hand.

'What's this?' Her tolerant, amused curiosity about my work was one of things I liked about her. One of them; there were plenty more. I gave her an abbreviated account of the case while she made some coffee. I didn't give her the details about the night with Erica, but I didn't need to—Hilde's antennae for sexual signals were highly tuned.

'What will Helen think about that?'

'What can she say? Do I object to her giving ol' Mike his conjugals?'

'You do, but you don't say. It's not quite the same, somehow.' She bent down and stroked the cat. 'He's sleek, looks like you're taking better care of him than yourself.'

'He runs the show. How's Frank?'

'He's fine, working hard what with all this hood-killing going on.' She patted her stomach and looked proudly at her big breasts. 'He's looking forward to it like mad. I hope he's there on the day.'

'He'll be there. I'm sorry, love. I've got to read this.'

'That's all right. If you find out any more, you can go on

143

with the story. I know you always keep back the nasty stuff anyway.'

I grinned. 'That's true.'

'I'll collect up some more of my junk. What happened here? Everything's all messed up.'

'I had visitors.'

'Nasty stuff.'

She went upstairs, and I turned my attention to the manuscript. The new sections were calculated to give Lambert cardiac arrest. He was right about the drive and intensity; Mountain seemed to be constructing the thing in a series of cliff-hangers, a series of climaxes building towards a grand climax as he drew the threads together and hurled characters into collision. The self-destructive theme, hinted at earlier, became an obsessive, schizophrenic battle heightened by drugs. I read with fascination, until I remembered that I was supposed to be reading for enlightenment and information about the writer. Even in its sketchy form the account of the social drug scene, and the woman the protagonist involved himself with, jelled with Artie Henderson's information. The woman had rape fantasies, and it appeared that the book would delve into her real life encounter with a would-be rapist and its effect on her sexual psychology. And on the hero's. Some of the language suggested that Mountain had read a bit in the field, or listened closely to Dr Holmes.

'Elizabeth Groves' was Deirdre Kelly and 'Morgan Shaw' was William Mountain, but who else was he?

I was re-reading intently when Hilde came back. She coughed politely.

'I've got to go, Cliff. How does it look now?'

'Bloody sticky. Didn't do any psychology along with the dentistry, did you, love?'

'Not much. Why?'

'Are schizophrenics suicidal, d'you reckon?'

'God, is it that heavy? I suppose so—some of them.'

'Know anything about rape fantasies?'

144

'Ugh, no. My fantasies are a lot more gentle.'

'You must tell me about them some time.'

'If you go first.' She hefted a bundle of clothes onto her hip as if she was practising for motherhood. I grinned at her.

'I'd have to think about that. Is Frank at work now?'

'Should be.' She blew me a kiss and went off down the passage. I missed her as soon as I heard the door close. I got my notebook and took it over to the phone.

'Parker.'

'Gidday, Frank, it's Hardy. I've just been talking to Hilde.'

'That puts you up on me, I haven't seen her for nearly twenty-four hours. Is she okay?'

'Never better. I need some help, Frank.'

'Jesus, Cliff. It's a bad time.'

'Quick file job. Policewoman Bennett could handle it.'

'She's moved to Vice. Never mind, I'll get someone. What is it?'

I told him as much as I needed to get the files checked and he said he'd get back to me in half an hour or sooner. That gave me time to make a sandwich and re-heat some of Hilde's coffee. I'd taken two bites and was adding the milk, when the phone rang; he's a fast worker, Frank, and he likes to have fast workers around him.

'There's not much on it,' he said.

'Anything.'

'Your voice sounds strange.'

'I'm chewing; excuse my manners. I promise I won't spit. I'm also drinking some coffee Hilde made for me.'

'That doesn't sound right; I'm at work and doing little chores for you and you're drinking my woman's coffee.'

'Don't worry about it. Just be eternally grateful to me for bringing you two together.'

'I am. Well, wanna hear it?'

I swallowed for an answer.

'Okay, Deirdre Kelly, age thirty-six, Montague Street,

West Pymble, lives alone, divorced, no kids, runs a travel agency in the city. Doing well, blah, blah. She alleged she was attacked in the car park ... quoting now, she presented with hysterical symptoms, unquote. She was a bit scratched up, nothing serious. Assailant had a knife, didn't want money. She didn't say what he *did* want.'

'How did she get clear?'

'Screamed the place awake, ran around a bit. A neighbour came out and helped her. Do you want the resident's name?'

'Is that the neighbour, the resident?'

'Yeah. God, I'm out of line giving you this.'

'Don't think I need the neighbour's name, or the resident's. Did this person see the attacker?'

'Ah ... no.'

'Who filed the report.'

'Christ, the signature's written in Martian. Constable Selwyn. He seems to be the one with the medical grasp, talks about contusions, would you believe.'

'What did he do?'

'Scouted the vicinity, interviewed a few residents ...'

'And?'

'Found nothing.'

'Action?'

'None. Only odd thing detected, and I use the word advisedly, by the alert Selwyn, was that Kelly said she'd driven herself home, but one of the residents had the impression that another car had come into the car park just before the ruckus.'

I grunted. 'Kelly sticks with "unknown assailant"?'

'Yep. Dr Selwyn has an opinion, of course. He opines that Kelly suffered a "hysterical fantasy", probably brought on by rejection.'

'He sounds like a useful bloke, save you a lot of work.'

'I don't know; work is what turns him on. He goes on to say that he thinks Kelly could be dangerous.'

'How's that?'

'Ah, she described the knife in detail and later said she wished she could have turned the knife on the ....'

'Alleged assailant.'

'Yeah, thank Christ the press didn't get hold of that.'

'Ah-hah,' I said, 'the fourth estate.'

'Yeah. Some reporter picked up the story. Probably got tipped off by a resident. There was a little piece in *The Globe* that tried to tie it in with a few other attacks up there, but it died. No good asking you what you're poking into I suppose?'

There was nothing to be accomplished just then by search warrants, arrests or formal charges. All the criminality—Mountain's, Grey's, possibly Kelly's, possibly my own—was relative. I thanked Frank, and said I'd see him soon. He heard notes in my voice I wasn't aware of.

'Be careful, Cliff. These are violent times.'

'All times are violent, but some times are more violent than others.'

'Just keep your head down. My kid needs an uncle.'

He rang off and I looked down at my notepad. I underlined Kelly's name and addressed and boxed it in; then I shaded around it; I drew a triangle on top of the box and cross-hatched the triangle. The doodle might have meant something to Dr Holmes but it didn't mean a damn thing to me.

20

PYMBLE is a long way off the track I beat. By reputation, it is inhabited by people who feel good about their big mortgages and tax shelters. They write letters to the papers about capital gains tax and abuses of the welfare system. It is a place light on pubs, corner shops and cars parked in the street—not one I had much impulse to visit, and especially now, with a hard Friday behind me, a phone call to make by midnight, and no very good ideas.

I had a shower and shave in honour of the money in Pymble, and I had a beer and put my gun in the holster under my armpit in honour of Glebe. I was wearing a blue cotton shirt and pants and a denim jacket Hilde had bought me. She said the style was blouson; I said it was good for concealing a gun.

The drive to Pymble took an hour plus. I had to battle against the North Shoreites who were coming into town for a good time. For company, I had the people who were going up to their hobby farms for the weekend. It was like struggling in a river of money with the current going both ways.

In the directory, West Pymble appears as part of the peninsula of residential land that sticks out into the green belt of the Lane Cove river park. The streets were tree-lined with wide, grassy strips outside the broad frontages. To the south, the park was like a dense, dark, whispering sea. The daylight was finished when I arrived at Montague Street, and excessive street lighting must have been considered vulgar in those parts, because I found myself squinting and peering through the gloom

148

trying to spot the apartment block.

I located it towards the end of the street; it was a new building, set back and masquerading as a hide-out in Sherwood Forest. The architect must have been given plenty of space to play with, because he'd arranged the three-storey structure around a courtyard with subsidiary gardens and discreet car parks. There were no obtrusive, high brick walls, no foot-high letters reading 'The Gables', no concrete patches for rubbish bins. It was all so pricey and in keeping with the stately houses in the street that the old-time residents couldn't have objected.

Kelly's address was Apartment Seven, another nice touch; no suggestion that there would ever be another apartment block here but this monument to good taste. I parked across the street and approached the entrance to what I was privately calling flat seven. I was behaving completely instinctively, with no plan, and only the vaguest idea of what I was looking for or what I might say.

The cars parked in the area that serviced numbers five to eight were a Honda Accord, a Ford Laser and a Citroën. One empty space; no Audi. Kelly's apartment had a basement section that took advantage of the sloping land; there were slanted windows, like skylights, to let light into it, on either side of the entrance to the ground floor section, which looked to comprise three bedrooms at least, with plenty of space around them. Patio at the back with French windows; side door letting out onto a flag-stoned path and vine-entwined pergola. Pretty nice if you could afford it, and didn't mind living this far from the GPO.

There were some lights showing in the apartment, and I thought I could hear a murmur of voices. I went under the pergola and took a peep up at a window; the junction boxes and cables indicated medium-heavy security. I went up the wide brick steps and banged on the door. Nothing happened to the lights or the voices. As I retreated to the steps, a car swung in off the road, mounted the grass at the side of the gravel path, found the path again and skidded into the courtyard. It was a silver VW with a soft top and a left hand drive; the driver swung the wheel hard at the last moment and the car ended up skew-whiff, half in and half out of the empty parking bay.

A woman got out of the car and flicked the door back behind her; the action caused her to over-balance and grab at the car for support. She was tall with long blonde hair. One tanned shoulder, that had either come free of her white dress or was meant to be free of it, gleamed under the dim courtyard light. She pushed off from the car, stumbled and dropped her keys. She giggled; then she bent and clawed the gravel. She stopped giggling and started swearing. I went down the steps, crossed the gravel and grass, bent and picked up her keys. She came up from her crouch reaching for them like a dog begging. She was pretty, with a sharp-featured face and big eyes.

'Thanks.' She took the keys and nearly dropped them again.

'You're not Deirdre Kelly, are you?'

'No, I'm not . . . . Hey, don't look so disappointed. That's not nice. Don't I look good enough?'

'You look fine. I wanted to see her, that's all.'

She swayed, and reached back for the fabric top of the car. 'Won't be home tonight. Tomorrow for sure.'

'How do you know—for sure?'

'Party, boy. Big party tomorrow. Hey, look, would you mind giving me a hand from here. I'm a bit pissed.' She leaned forward to take a closer look at me, lost her balance and grabbed my shoulders. She dropped the keys again. 'Not an attacker 'r anything like that, 're you?' She smelled of gin, perfume and tobacco. 'Don't look like attacker. Look like a pilot or something. You a pilot?'

'No,' I said. I bent down for the keys, got an arm around her and helped her take a few faltering steps on her four inch heels. 'Which way?'

She pointed a long, slim arm at number eight, and I

half-carried her along the path and up the steps. She leaned against the wall by the doorway and took off her shoes. I held out the keys.

'Oh no, no, no,' she slurred. 'You don't leave little Ginny like that. C'mon in and have a drink. You open the door, I couldn't get it in.'

She did some more giggling while I opened the door; I held it wide, and she tossed her shoes inside.

'C'm in.'

I was still half-supporting her, and it was beginning to be a job. She was slim, but five feet ten or so of slim, drunk woman is still a fair weight. We went down a thick-carpeted hall towards a light burning dimly in the distance. It turned out to be a kitchen light shining through a smoked glass door. I pulled at the door with my temporarily free hand; she giggled and pushed.

The kitchen was new and glowing. It was one of those things you buy in a package and have installed by a team of men in T-shirts who sing snatches from Gilbert & Sullivan while they work. Ginny supported herself on the bench that divided the room and then made a gliding lunge for a chair set up beside a big, circular pine table. She hit it hard; the chair creaked but held.

'Get a drink,' she croaked. 'What d'you like?'

'Wine.'

'Me too. Champagne in the fridge.'

There were several bottles of assorted good brands in the refrigerator. I pulled out the nearest, found some glasses and a tea towel and joined her at the table.

''s good stuff. I want fizz.'

She jumped at the pop of the cork and giggled. I poured a full glass for me and a half for her. She smiled loosely, drained the glass in a gulp and held it out for more. I poured again and took a mouthful of the crisp bubbles. She lifted her glass and drained it again.

'Toast to me,' she said. 'Toast to Ginny Ireland.'

'Ireland?'

'Like the place. Oh, can't toast, glass's empty.'

I filled her up. 'You sound like an American.'

'Was. Aussie now, married an' divorced an Aussie. What's your name?'

'Cliff.'

'Cheers, Cliffy.'

We drank some more. Her big, dark eyes started to take on a faraway look, and I reckoned that the time I had left to question her could be measured in millilitres. 'Will you be going to Deirdre's party, Ginny?'

'Sure, always go to Dee's. You goin', Cliffy?'

'I haven't got an invitation, I'd like to see Dee though. Got some business to discuss among other things.'

'Sounds boring, but I guess you're sorta in the same business.'

I didn't say anything but let her ramble on until I could pick up my cues. After some hiccupping, it became clear that she'd fixed on the idea that I was an airline pilot. I let her run with that, and agreed with her that I'd be retiring soon and had to look after myself. That seemed to satisfy her in the way of a connection with Deirdre Kelly. She up-ended the bottle and watched it drip into her glass. I had a hand ready to catch it, but she set it down with the excessive carefulness drunks have at this stage.

'She's okay, Dee. She's okay, I don' care what they say.'

'Who says what?'

She bent her head to lap at the brim full glass. Strands of her hair fell in the wine and she let them drift into her mouth where she sucked them. She'd drunk nearly two thirds of the bottle on top of the load she already had, and her gaiety was dimming into something slow and studied. 'Say she's crazy, say she 'magines things that don't really happen.'

'What do you think?'

The gloss was peeling off her fast. Sweat beaded her face and the wet strands of hair were dark and matted; the make-up around her eyes was smeared and her nose was shiny under the bright kitchen light. 'Everybody makes up things. I do. You do, doncha?'

'I suppose so.'

'Course you do. Dee's friends've got no right saying things 'bout her like that. Bet they make up things.'

'Sure. Be interesting to meet a few of 'em, guess what they'd make up.'

She banged her fist on the table. 'Hey, you're right. Like a party game: what're your make-believes, bet I c'n guess.' In her new mood the whim was taking on a solid reality. 'Less do it.'

I grinned and sipped.

'Less do it tomorrow night. Lots there. You can come with me, Cliffy. Be fun.'

I nodded. Her eyes, which had been sliding around the room trying to find something to focus on, finally held on my face for an instant. Her head came forward in a disjointed imitation of my nod, but the movement kept on and her forehead hit the table with a light thud. She twitched once and passed out.

I sipped the rest of my wine and waited until her shoulders had slumped and she was breathing regularly. Then I prowled through the big apartment. Her bedroom was furnished in the same packaged style as the kitchen with matching double bed, built-in cupboards and dressing table. There were enough clothes to outfit Charlie's Angels and none of them was cheap. The fur on the pile of cushions on the bed looked real. Other rooms held basic furniture and there was no indication of where the funds came from.

I turned on a soft light by the bed, peeled the covers back to the black silk sheets and shoved some pillows into place. Back in the kitchen I located some aspirin and put them with a glass of water on the table by the bed. Ginny had slipped forward and was in danger of ending up under the table, literally. I picked her up, carried her to the bed and set her down. She stirred briefly and grabbed a

pillow. On a sheet torn from my notebook I wrote:
'Looking forward to the party. I'll be here around nine.
Love, Cliff.' I added a quick and not too inaccurate sketch
of an airline pilot's wings to the bottom of the note,
because I thought Ginny's visual recall might be better
than her verbal.

I put her keys on the bedside table, and her shoes neatly
together in the hall. I turned off a few lights and thought I
could hear a light snoring as I let myself out of the
apartment.

21

Nothing had changed at number seven, no new lights, no new cars outside; professional pride didn't impel me to identify the TV channel that was providing the voices. I drove back to Glebe with the slip of paper on which I'd written the midnight contact number in my jacket pocket. I kept feeling the paper as I drove, wishing it was something more substantial, wishing that I was causing things to happen instead of being Grey's representative in Mountain's game.

I got home with a couple of minutes to spare. I dialled and got a recorded message as I expected. It told me to speak after the blip.

Blip. 'This is Hardy, Grey. I think I'm onto something but the relevant meeting is tomorrow night. Don't hurt the girl or I swear I'll come after you and break your back. I assume you'll be in touch.' I hung up feeling ridiculous at making threats into machines at the stroke of midnight. I waited. At five minutes into the new day the phone rang and the same voice as before spoke quickly: 'Delighted to hear that you're making progress. The girl is fine, although we've had some trouble in restraining Peroni. Don't made empty threats. Hardy; it creates a bad impression. I'm going to read you your next contact number twice. I'll expect a call twenty-four hours from now.' He did that, I wrote the number down and the line went dead.

There are more ways to set up secure telephone contacts than there are to nobble horses and the Grey Organisation (as I'd come to think of it) seemed to be aware of it. I sat and brooded, forseeing a series of nights of telephone calls until there was nothing on the other end of the line. The thought chilled and depressed me. I went to bed where I had trouble finding sleep, and when I did find it, the sleep was troubled by dreams of Helen Broadway, Erica Fong and bloody objects arriving in the mail.

About ten the following morning, I got a call from Terry Reeves. The Audi had been found.

'God,' I said. 'Where?'

'Right outside the office.'

'In what condition?'

'Mint. You have anything to do with this, Cliff?'

'Mate, I'd like to claim the credit, but I can't. I've been on the trail of the bloke who took it, but I haven't even got close to him. I *think* he's in Sydney—that's how it's been, that vague.'

He grunted. 'Well, I'm not complaining. Send me an account and I'll fix you up.'

'Okay.' I was embarrassed; it felt like taking money for nothing and I went in for some self-justificaton. 'Terry, there's an organisation behind this; it goes interstate . . . .'

'I'm not madly interested, Cliff. Not very public-spirited of me, I know, but I've got a business to run. Unless you're saying it could happen to me again?'

'I don't know.'

'Are you saying you can recover the other cars, mine I mean?'

'No.'

'I think we'll call it a day then, Cliff. Thanks for what you've done. I can wear the insurance on the others, the Audi would have been the last straw.'

He was embarrassed, too. We both went polite and let each other off lightly, the way friends should. I'd keep my bill low, and he'd pay promptly. The Crusades were a long time ago. The business situation—left with no new client and inhibitions about billing the last one—was bad, but the side issues the Reeves case had generated threatened to be a disaster. I didn't know where Erica was, or what Mountain was doing by returning the car. That was puzzling. Did it mean that Mountain had been in touch with Grey and that this was a move in that game? Would Grey have told Mountain about Erica, and what would Mountain's reaction be? It was like fumbling around in a dark, locked room for a light switch that wasn't there.

I knocked up a cheapo bill for Terry and drove to Darlinghurst feeling worm-like. The orange skirts and white blouses blossomed around the parking bays and in the office, and the place seemed to wear a new air of optimism. I walked into the office with the folded account in my hand, wanting to explain the circumstances, but wanting to meet Terry Reeves about as much as I wanted to meet Pol Pot.

Things had changed a bit. Terry's office was now a walled-in box. That was probably the idea of some security consultant; there seemed to be more screens around too—TV monitors and VDTs. Terry wouldn't like the changes, but maybe he didn't have any choice. His secretary was parked outside his office behind a big desk with an intricate-looking telephone system. In her quick glance I read approval of the new arrangement and disapproval of me. She held out her hand for the paper I was carrying.

'Mr Reeves isn't in,' she said.

'Cliff Hardy.'

'I'm sorry, Mr Hardy, he *really* isn't in.'

I handed the account across. 'This is my account for the work I've been doing for him. I understand the Audi has been returned?'

'Yes.'

'I'd like to look at it, please.'

She looked doubtful. 'I don't know . . .'

'I don't want to dismantle or drive it, I just want a look. It's important.'

She wasn't going to budge. 'What would you be looking for?'

'I don't know, anything that might have been left in it.' I opened my hands. 'Evidence.'

'I see.' She picked up her phone and dialled the workshop. If the CIA had had her, Chris Boyce would still be flying falcons. She spoke briefly into the phone and looked up at me. 'Are you interested in body damage?'

'Only to me.'

She tapped her pencil impatiently and I nodded. She spoke again and looked up. 'There isn't any. They're sending up everything they found. Mr Reeves asked for it to be kept.'

'Thank you.' She motioned me to a seat and I sat down feeling grateful that Reeves' old investigative habits were still with him. The secretary got on with her phoning and filing and ignored me; I was very low on charisma for the employees of Bargain Renta Car. After a while a man in orange overalls came into the office and put a plastic bag on the secretary's desk.

'Thanks, Ken.'

Ken winked at her and went out. She pushed the bag across the desk and I reached for it. Inside was a tattered copy of the Melbourne *Age*, a half-empty bottle of Suntory whisky and a glossy, folded pamphlet. The secretary's eyes widened as I unfolded the pamphlet; mine probably widened too. It was a catalogue of sadomasochistic 'love aids' available from the I'll Be Bound boutique in the Cross. Whips, light and heavy; leather constraints of various kinds; chains; velvet and silk garments designed to define areas of interest. The stuff was superbly photographed and the whole production had a streamlined, high-tech gloss. The chains gleamed against velvet folds; the whip ends lay on smooth, soft leather. There were lavish bedroom scenes in which the faces and bodies of

the active and passive participants were taut with pleasure.

The secretary got up and came around her desk for
a better look. She gazed over my shoulder at a picture
of a black man with an enormous erection and wearing
a white mask who was shackling a couple who were in
a contortionistic oral embrace.

'God,' she said.

'Turn you on?'

'I don't know.'

I folded up the pamphlet and put it in my pocket. She
was breathing hard but still at her post. 'I don't know that
you should take that away.'

'I'm old enough,' I said. I put the paper and bottle back
in the bag. 'Here, you can give this to Ken.'

22

THE Falcon sometimes won't start unless you jiggle the key in a certain way, and I sometimes forget to jiggle the key if I'm not concentrating on starting the car. The starter motor was whining and the engine wasn't firing as I tried to remember the phrase Lambert had used of Morgan Shaw. 'New interest', that was it. That resolved, I jiggled the key and the car started.

The I'll Be Bound boutique was one floor up above a doctor's surgery in Bayswater Road. It was elegantly appointed, all deep-carpet and muted-light chic. The goods were on display in discreetly under-lit glass cases with heavy un-chic locks. The staff consisted of two people, rail-thin with deathly pale faces, wearing black tights and jumpers and dark make-up, who could have been of either sex or neither. I blinked in the gloom and one of them approached me and asked if he or she could be of any help.

'I don't know,' I said. I pulled out the pamphlet and put it down on a glass case, covering a red and black silk nightie and knicker set that would be no use at all on a cold winter night. 'Can anyone get hold of one of these or are they for special customers only?'

The person swivelled on a medium heel and pointed at the counter which I could scarcely see through the gloom. 'They are over there. Anyone can come in and take one.'

'I see.' I peered at the counter and saw something above it that looked like a cross-bow before I realised it was a double dildo with ribbons. There was a stack of the pamphlets beside a silk top hat. 'Yes, I see.'

A man wearing a yellow jump suit came into the shop

and the attendant's black-rimmed eyes flicked across to him. 'Is there anything else, sir?'

'No, thank you.'

'Look around. You might see something you like.'

I felt my way across to the counter; a woman came out from behind a curtain wearing a leather vest with holes in it that allowed her breasts to poke out. She looked at me.

'What d'you think?' she said.

'Great,' I said.

The other attendant sniffed; I grabbed another copy of the pamphlet and groped my way back to the stairs.

I stopped in Glebe to buy the sort of shampoo and aftershave that would go with a swinging party in Pymble. Driving home, I tried to remember the last party I'd been to. I recalled a couple Helen and I had dropped in on for an hour or less, and one good one that had celebrated the birthday of an FM disc jockey neighbour. We'd all got drunk and sung the songs of the sixties. I doubted there'd be much Buddy Holly sung in Pymble.

I cleaned myself up, ate and drank something and tried to feel professional. It was hard without a client. I re-read the Mountain synopsis, or bits of it, but there was no indication of what Morgan Shaw's 'new interest' might be—it could have been sado-masochism, it could've been stamp collecting. The cat followed me around the house. Every time I turned around it was there, looking at me. I fed it and it still followed me. I put it outside and it jumped up to the window and looked in at me.

'I didn't cut your balls off,' I said. 'It happened long before we met.' The cat seemed satisfied with that; it stretched out to sleep in what was left of the afternoon sun.

At 3pm Dr Holmes telephoned me. 'Mr Hardy,' he said. 'Something rather strange has happened.'

'You've seen Mountain?'

'No, no. A cheque has arrived covering the cost of all his sessions to date, including the last one which he missed.'

'No letter?'

'No—a cheque in an envelope. There's a strange air of finality to it. I thought I'd give you a call to see if you'd learned anything further.'

A strange air of finality, I thought. It sounded like something to take to the ESP consultant in my corridor.

'Hardy, are you there?'

'Yes, sorry, Doctor. I've got some news of him, none of it good.' I gave him a run-down on the progress of William Mountain as I'd followed it to that point. He clicked his tongue at the references to self-destruction; the sound came across the wire and hurt my ear.

'That's very disturbing. Could you find a typical phrase on that sort of point in the manuscript?'

I had the synopsis in front of me along with my notebook and my two I'll Be Bound catalogues. I flicked through the typescript. 'Here's a good bit: quote: "I would like to consume myself, cannibalise myself, starting with the brain", unquote. How's that?'

'I hope you are taking this seriously.'

'I am. Believe me. I'm expecting to meet up with him sooner or later, and I'm not looking forward to it.'

'I wouldn't be too sure about that meeting. He'd be capable of swift self-destruction if the schizophrenia is as extreme as it appears from your account.'

'Thanks a lot.'

'Do you have any other observations, other signs of distress?'

'You name it—heroin, cocaine, abstinence from alcohol.' I fidgeted with the things on the table and my hand touched the pamphlet. 'Oh, yes, it could be that he's into SM—bondage, discipline, whips and chains, that sort of stuff.'

'That's dangerous, very dangerous. In his heightened emotional state he could do terrible damage to himself and others.'

'What about this book he's writing? How do you see that in the scheme of things?'

'That's worrying too. There are so many associations— book as child, book as life force, book as legacy. Are you following me?'

'I think so. He could equate finishing the book with finishing his life.'

'It's possible. It's urgent that he be found.'

'If I find him and he seems to be crazy, can I bring him to you first?'

'It would depend on what he'd done.'

'What if he'd done the worst things that you and I can think of?'

He paused and I could imagine his burly body tense with concentration while his workman's hands were busy with pencil and pad. 'Of course you must bring him to me. I'll give you my private number.' He did, and I wrote it down. 'Do you expect to catch up with him soon?'

'Soon or never, from what you say, Doctor. Will this number get you anytime over the next couple of days?'

He said it would, and I rang off feeling that, somehow, the stakes had mounted, the pot had got bigger and my hand had stayed the same. That feeling intensified when I finally got through to Grant Evans in Melbourne. I could sense Grant's reluctance to talk on an open line in the police building, and our conversation became cryptic, but we were both used to that.

'It's tip of the iceberg stuff, Cliff.'

'I thought it might be. The cars are a sideline to ... what?'

'Insurance fraud, among other things. Look, I can't talk on this line.'

I knew what was coming: the old, old story of organisa-tions closing ranks to protect members no matter how undeserving. Grant interpreted my silence correctly. 'Look, Cliff,' he said angrily. 'It's not just that. I remember

one of your rules, what was it? Never knowingly work for
. . .'

I completed the phrase for myself—*politicians and
unions*. Again, Grant knew what I was thinking.

'Precisely,' he said. 'Keep out of it, Cliff.'

For the rest of the afternoon I divided my time between
looking through Mountain's manuscript, re-reading some
letters Helen had sent me and staring at the sleeping cat.
Phrases from Mountain's writing began to etch themselves on my mind: *Most people only get half-fucked,
half-drunk and half-drugged. It's hard work going all the
way.*

It struck me that perhaps Lambert was wrong—
Mountain's synopsis had energy and violence and sex, but,
as I read and re-read, I detected a lack of humour. Death,
drugs and sex can be as funny as anything else, properly
handled, and I thought I could recall a few good laughs in
The Godfather. It would be the final irony if Bill Mountain's possibly posthumous book was a flop.

I tried to imagine myself in his place. It wasn't easy.
Somewhere, he was sitting writing the thing, stone cold
sober or drugged to the hairline. He had plans, maybe a
major, double-edged strategy with fall-back positions.
He'd covered a lot of ground in a very short time, and
there was something single-minded and purposeful in his
actions. He'd left clues and was aware of being pursued.
In the book, Morgan Shaw saw his pursuers as the car
thieves and drug dealers whom he'd offended by moving
in on their areas of operation. He harried the one and
eluded the other; shut himself up and worked on his film
script. No jokes. I shut up the folder and shoved it under a
telephone directory. That dislodged an ashtray which
spilled Erica's butts and ash on the floor. The tobacco and
ash smelled stale and old—that wasn't funny either.
Another Shaw/Mountain gem came back to me: *I was
ready to kill myself, and I felt so good about taking this
control over my own life that I was only sorry that I
hadn't had anything to do with being born.*

164

23

I WAS wearing the same outfit as before when I rang the bell at Ginny Ireland's apartment, except that my shirt was clean, and I had the gun in a holster inside my pants around the back from my left hip. The bulge would show if I took my jacket off, but from what I'd seen of parties lately there was hardly enough light to see the cheese dip so a slight gun bulge wouldn't be a problem.

Ginny opened the door and hurled herself through it, at me. I got her strong arms around my neck and a smacking kiss that almost put me down for a count. She was wearing red high heels, tight red pants and a blouse that looked to be made of gold leaf. She hauled me into the apartment.

'You yummy man, yummy, yummy. That was so *sweet* of you last night. Most men would've ... well, thank you.'

I waved my hand modestly and followed her through to the kitchen, where the gin fumes were competing with the sweet smell of marijuana. She picked up a long, fat joint, re-lit it and held it out to me after inhaling deeply herself.

I picked up the Beefeater bottle. 'Later,' I said. 'I'll start on this.'

'Lush.' She poured a hefty slug of gin, splashed in some tonic and just hit the rim of the glass with a slice of lemon so that the lemon dropped in. Then she forgot to give me the glass. I reached over and took it.

She giggled. 'I was so smashed last night, and I'm telling you when I woke up and saw that aspirin and that water, boy, I'd have given you anything you wanted, there and then.'

I grinned. 'Well, as I say, later.'

She seemed to find that the funniest thing she'd ever

heard. She laughed and choked on her next drag. I patted her on the back, gently so as not to tear the gold leaf. Up close there was a synthetic quality to her that was dimmed by distance. Her hair was dyed and the big eyes were a product of pencil and brush more than something nature had given her. The skin along her jaw was beginning to sag and last night's session had left slight pouches under her eyes that would deepen as she ran one good time into the next.

We finished our drinks and she went off to add some more touches to the art work. When she came back she smelled strongly and freshly of the perfume that had gone stale on her last night.

'Okay, Cliffy?'

I pointed to the bag of grass on the kitchen bench. 'Not taking the dope?'

She laughed. 'To one of Dee's parties? You must be joking. She'd be insulted.'

We trooped across to number seven. A big man in a white jacket and dark pants was standing by the door trying to look like a guest, but succeeding in looking like a bouncer. Ginny smiled at him and he gave her a quick nod, me a hard stare, and opened the door. The noises and smells hit like a head-high tackle: insistent, driving rock music, a rush of voices and thick, spicy smoke. The apartment was similarly laid out to Ginny Ireland's, except that the decor was more flamboyant: polished boards with tiger skins in the hall and woven beaded hangings on the wall that showed erotic scenes in a certain amount of strategic relief. The party was being held in a big double room with the dividing cedar doors thrown back: the ceilings were mostly mirrored as were the walls; the floor was a deep white cloud and there were two conversation pits, a number of low poufs covered with animal skins and a couple of things that looked like trampolines but were probably couches. In one corner of the room there was a well-stocked bar. The topless attendant wore high heels and fishnet stockings and also had the job of feeding cassettes into the huge Sony tape deck.

About thirty people stood or lounged around talking, drinking, smoking, looking at themselves in the mirrors. A few swayed to the music; others just swayed. Ginny led me over to the bar, where there were a couple of shallow silver dishes filled with white powder; there was a tiny gold spoon on a long chain attached to each dish. Ginny dipped and conveyed the spoon to her nose with a rock steady hand.

'Your motto seems to be fun is for later, Cliffy.' She sniffed the powder up one nostril. 'Mine's fun is for now!' She took a cigarette out of a box on the bar, held it for the attendant to light, puffed and drifted away. I looked along the bar at the dishes of powder and the bowls of grass with papers and filters; there were also little silver pill boxes and some small glass phials set out on pads of crushed velvet.

The barmaid's nipples were painted black and she had some trouble keeping them out of the work area. Her eyes were bright and glittering under gold-dusted lashes.

'Care for something?'

'Water,' I said.

She looked confused and took one long black-painted fingernail to her mouth. 'I'm sorry, we haven't . . .'

'I was kidding. I'll have a gin and tonic, light on the gin.'

She made the drink quickly and expertly and selected a long, silver cylinder from under the bar. 'Care for a dash?'

I shook my head, took the drink and looked around for something to look at. The room was filling up fast, and I concluded that there must be other comfort stations in the apartment, because people came in through the doors with glasses full and joints aglow. I went out a door, after pausing in front of it to make sure it really *was* a door. The music and smoke, from other speakers and other throats, followed me down to the kitchen and into other rooms. The whole place was dark, and the decor gave it a dreamy, insubstantial quality: dark walls with deliberately shadowy corners, mirrors and leather and fibreglass furniture that seemed to writhe where it stood. Nothing was rectangular; day beds and divans were oval; the bath was a modular unit you had to dive into and curl up in; the toilet was a series of hoses with attachments moulded to fit the different private parts. One door off the main hallway was locked.

When I got back under the mirrored ceilings, the party was beginning to swing: the music was louder and the people seemed to be laughing more, and coming more often into minor physical collisions. In one corner a group of men in dinner suits had formed a sort of rugby line-out and was tossing a small woman aloft and passing her from hand to hand. A man in a long white caftan was dancing with a woman in a tail coat and all the fittings, and two women who looked like twins in identical lamé dresses were inspecting a selection of their images in a mirrored corner.

I spotted Ginny through the murk, and went over to her. She was smashed to bits, but still riding high with energy and alertness. She grabbed my arm and we almost tumbled together down into one of the conversation pits.

'Dee,' she said, 'here's this *fabulous* man, Cliff somebody.'

'Hello, somebody.' Deirdre Kelly was a long, dark woman wearing a long, dark dress. She had black shiny hair and a creamy white skin. The dress left her, slim arms bare; she had wide expanding metal bands around her upper arms and metal bracelets around her wrists. When she moved her arms the muscles rippled and swelled like Lothar's. I smiled at her and said something about it being an interesting party, while I waited for Ginny to drop me right in by saying I had business with her. But that information had dropped out for Ginny long ago; she got up to dance with a Jamaican in stretch jeans, who called her 'Sugar' and whose idea of dancing was to spread his big hands over her buttocks and press her hard into where the denim bulged the most.

Dee Kelly saw me watching the performance and frowned. 'You seem a little out of place here, somebody.'

'Why d'you say that?'

She reached for a silver dish and used the gold spoon expertly. She dipped and held it out to me. I shook my head. She smiled and took a brown cigarette from a box. I shook my head again. She took one of the little phials and held it between thumb and forefinger.

'No again, huh?'

I nodded.

She took a disposable syringe from a pocket in her dress and pulled off the plastic caps from both ends. 'See what I mean?' She suddenly jabbed the needle into my thigh and pressed the plunger. I jumped and swore. She laughed. 'You don't fit in. what brings you here?'

I plucked the needle out and broke off the short, thin, metal spike. 'What was that?'

'Nothing. Water. Just a joke.' She gripped my arm and pulled; I was struggling to get up but she seemed strangely strong. 'Relax, relax.'

I didn't relax; I felt frozen and dumb. 'Ginny brought me.'

'I know *that*! She's stupid enough to do anything.'

'Stupid?' I got my thick tongue around the word and idea. 'Stupid? Living like this? Having all this fun?'

She gave me a look that would have cut glass. Her face was boldly made up as if to be photographed or seen from a distance. Up close there was a grossness to her features: wide pores, large ears under the shiny hair and a suggestion of bad breath. Her mouth was loose and moist and she kept it that way by frequent use of her tongue which was purplish from contact with her lipstick. I sat down, heavily.

'She's stupid, all right,' she said. 'If you needed brains for fucking, she'd be a virgin.' The aphorism seemed to please her; she leaned back and stretched. She had heavy, full breasts which rose and pushed out the front of her dark silk dress. She saw me looking and licked her lips, then she dipped the spoon again and sniffed the stuff down to her ankles.

I thought: *Half-fucked, half-drunk, half-drugged.* Dee Kelly was going all the way; she closed her eyes for a full minute and when she opened them they were alert and shrewd, beacons of her brain. 'I'll ask you again,' she said. 'Why are you here?'

English suddenly seemed like a foreign language to me. 'To see Bill Mountain,' I said thickly.

The name jolted her although she tried to hide the reaction. A sort of tremor ran the full, long length of her, and she drew her knees up and closed her eyes in a spasm.

'Who did you say?'

The lassitude dropped away. Now I felt bright and chatty, communicative and in control. 'William Mountain. He's an amazing man. He's writing a novel—and you're in it, Mrs Kelly, in a starring role.'

She threw back her head and laughed in a sharp cackle. 'Mrs Kelly! God, it's been years since anyone called me that. What else d'you know about me?'

'I don't know anything about you and I don't want to know anything. But I think you'll lead me to Mountain.'

'What's your business with him?'

The music was louder still, and the party noise was mounting to a roar. I had to lean close to her to be heard, and that rank smell got stronger. 'That's between him and me. My feeling is he's going to be here tonight and I'm sticking close to you just in case you've got some idea of warning him off. You could call your watchdog in from the door, but the noise we'd make between us'd finish off your party.'

'I'm among friends here.'

I looked around the room: everyone I could see was

drunk or stoned or both. A couple of the men looked big enough to be useful but one of them was just starting to slide down the wall and another man was staring into his own eyes in the wall mirror. I felt I could move very fast if I had to; I didn't want to, but ... if I had to.

'I can't see anyone here who'd give me too much trouble,' I said, 'and there doesn't have to be any trouble in this for you. I just want to talk to Mountain when he comes. I hope I can make him see reason; if I can't, some things might get broken but I'll try to watch out for your mirrors.'

'I've never heard such crap. Get the hell out of here!'

She started to get up and I got a grip on her biceps around the bracelet and pulled here down. She flexed the muscle and resisted, but I put on more pressure. 'Listen, lady. I don't give a fuck what drugs you peddle to who. I don't care if you turn on the whole North Shore. I just want to see Mountain.'

She sneered at me, and the frustration and anger that had been bottled up in me for days came out; I needed to hurt someone and she was closest. I gripped her arm tighter. 'I don't care if you imagine people raping you and report it to the police. You can imagine me raping you if you like.'

She smiled suddenly and almost sweetly. It was as if I'd said the magic word. She tapped my hand with one long finger and I let her go. 'That's better,' she said. 'I've decided that you're an interesting man after all. Let me get you a drink.'

'You're not going anywhere.' I spoke in what I thought was a firm voice, but I felt less dominant, and anchored to the spot.

'No, no, of course.' She waved in the direction of the bar and made a gesture with her hands to indicate a drink. It was okay by me; my throat was dry from the heat and the smoke, and Deirdre Kelly's bad smell and sudden switch in mood had strung me out and made me nervous. The topless barmaid came over with a bottle of champagne and a glass on a tray. The party seethed around her, and she had to lift the tray to get it clear of grasping hands. Kelly cleared a hand aside with a swift chop and stroked a fish-netted thigh as she took the tray in her other hand.

'Not bad, eh? What d'you think of her?'

'She's well-built,' I said. 'When's Mountain due?'

'He'll be along.' She dismissed the barmaid with a light slap and poured me out a glass of champagne. 'I won't do anything to stop you seeing Bill, on one condition.'

I didn't answer; I didn't fancy bargaining with her. I drank some champagne and looked at the angry red mark I'd made on her arm. I felt a burning in my stomach— champagne's not what it was.

'On condition that you let me listen to your conversation.' She took the glass from me and sipped; her lipstick purpled the edge.

'That'd be up to him.'

'Oh, *he'd* let me. He lets me do anything I like.'

A man fell into the pit, and Kelly eased herself away from him and closer to me. There seemed to be just as many people in the room as before, but fewer of them were standing up.

'When did you see him last?'

'Today. This morning.' She leaned closer and her odour was gamy, feral. 'We made love all night.'

'That so? When does he find time to write?'

She laughed, not the cackle this time but a fluid, oily sound. 'Not when he's with me, I can promise you that. His writing's brilliant, like his fucking.'

'Have you read it?'

'No, but he's told me about it.'

I knew she was lying, and she knew I knew. She took the glass, drank some wine and spilled some more on her dress. The stain showed black on the dark silk.

'Consume myself, starting with my own brain.' I sounded like Orson Welles. I smiled and said it again.

'What?' she gasped.

'What?'

'You said something.' She shoved aside the man who had fallen into the pit and had rolled over. An arm flopped down from floor level and hung in space between us.

'No, I didn't say anything.' I looked around the room for the nearest door, just in case of trouble, but there was no door. The mirror ran from the ceiling and down all four walls. I blinked and the mirror shattered into a kaleidoscope of colours that blinked back at me. The people changed into dwarfs and giants; I tried to focus on the nearest faces and the features went rubbery and all shapes went angular like in a Picasso painting. A huge nose grew out of a man's rubbery face and pressed towards a woman's swollen breasts. Then the breasts shrank and the woman's chest went concave and the nose pressed in and in.

I tried to stand up but Deirdre Kelly pushed me down like a mother cat tumbling one of her kittens. The music shrilled and screamed; I put my hands over my ears to shut it out, and my ears felt huge, wet and terrifying. Kelly's rank breath flooded over me.

'You're passing out, Mr Somebody. You're going to be sorry you hurt me.'

I was sorry already, and wanted to say so. My stomach lurched and my head fell towards my knees and I didn't care where it landed. It passed my knees and went on falling.

24

W<small>HEN</small> I came out of it, I felt as if I was lying around in four or five separate pieces. Reconstituting myself was agony but I made the effort. I wriggled and twitched and made mental contact with the furthest off bits. When I was back in one piece I found that the piece was tied at the wrists and ankles. I was naked and in a room I had never seen before. That made for a very uncomfortable feeling, the familiarity of my body and the utter strangeness of the room.

If I was still in Apartment Seven, this had to be the locked room off the hallway. It wasn't hard to see why Dee Kelly kept it locked: the room was painted black from floor to ceiling; there was enough concealed lighting for me to make out objects in the room from the propped-against-a-wall position I'd wriggled into. A big low bed dominated one corner; a couple of upholstered chairs were over by one wall and there was a six foot high padded post jutting up out of the black carpet in the centre of the room. I squirmed to get my head around for a look along the wall. There seemed to be irregularities in it, protuberances that broke up the smooth, black surface. They were irregulares all right—chains and manacles in a dull, non-reflective metal like night-fighting weapons. I looked with alarm-sharpened vision at the bed; it had ropes and chains attached to its headboard; along another wall was a rack containing whips and canes and other objects I couldn't identify and didn't want to.

My arms were drawn together under my thighs and my wrists were tied; I was sitting with my knees drawn up and the knots of the ropes around my ankles were underneath, below my calves. When I could move my hands without wanting to scream, I tried to get my fingers to work on the knots, but it was impossible. No give in the rope—expert job. I had a raging thirst and could still hear, through the throbbing inside my head, the sounds I'd heard before I'd passed out, although I was pretty sure that the room was actually dead quiet. At least things were restored to their normal shapes and sizes, if you could say that bondage beds and chains and manacles had normal shapes and sizes.

I was registering these comforting, orientating thoughts when a section of black wall swung in and William Mountain entered the room. I recognised him, although he was incredibly changed. He was clean-shaven with short hair. Drastic weight loss had left the skin of his face loose and plastic-looking. His body was strong and well-conditioned; there could be no doubt about that, because all he was wearing was a pair of skin-tight leather pants.

He came across and looked down at me; his eyes were wide open, red-veined and mad. Those eyes were the most frightening thing so far in ten minutes or so of rising fear. He squatted down easily in front of me, and the fat lines around his waist were minimal. The light leather creaked.

'Cliff Hardy, how nice to see you.' His smile was simple, unaffected, genuine. I'd never seen him smile out of an un-hirsute face before, and the effect was obscene.

'Mountain,' I croaked. 'Great joke, Bill.'

He shook his head slowly. 'No joke, Hardy.'

'We've got a lot of talking to do,' I babbled. 'I've been looking for you for ...'

'Days, weeks, I know.'

'You know? How? Look, these bloody ropes're ...'

'I didn't exactly know it'd be *you*! I'm a bit surprised, actually. I thought you only did clean work, or cleanish. This is a dirty job—working for *them*.'

'I'm working for the guy you stole the cars from.'

His tongue flicked out and worked at the corner of his

mouth; I realised that he was trying to perform the old nervous trick of trapping a beard hair in his teeth and pulling it out with a movement of his head. The tongue moved uselessly. 'That's what the other one said.'

'You mean the guy at Blackheath?'

'You *have* been on the trail, Cliff. Congratulations on reaching the end.'

I summoned up some breath and saliva to enable me to speak clearly and keep the fear down. 'Let's not piss around, Mountain. You're in big, big trouble, but it's probably not too late to pull something out of this mess.'

He laughed then; the basso I'd heard in pubs and in his house; it was a warm, rich, totally good-humoured sound, and so inappropriate in that chamber of horrors that it had the effect of making me shiver. 'I've been on a journey,' he said easily. 'An incredible journey, the like of which no man has ever been on before.'

'Bullshit! You're talking half-baked mysticism, and you've been acting out fantasies half the men in Sydney share. Quit before you go too far.'

'You wouldn't understand. After all those years of seeing life through the bottom of a bottle, I've finally acted, I've finally freed myself. I've broken the block; I can write again.'

My full-frontal approach hadn't produced much of a result. Time for the soft-soap? 'Good for you,' I said. 'I know you've been writing. Your agent thinks it's wonderful.'

'So he should, it *is* wonderful. I slaved over that, it's Art!' Something happened to his eyes, which had been fixed directly on me, as he spoke. They seemed to wander away to focus on the remote distance. He put his hand up to stroke his face; his skin had lost its elasticity, and the flesh moved under his hand and moved back to its original shape only slowly. He unsquatted with the suggestion of an effort; he was still a heavy, bulky man, and walked out of the room. I shouted as he went but he didn't seem to hear me.

After a few minutes, he came back with Deirdre Kelly. She was wearing spike heeled, thigh-high boots, a G-string and a velvet jerkin that propped up her breasts and left them exposed. The sounds in my head had stopped, and in the few seconds that the door was open I registered that the party was over.

Mountain's eyes were back to red, wide and crazed again, and he was smiling.

'I promised Dee I'd let her hear this.'

'I'm glad you keep your promises,' I said. 'It makes me feel more at home.'

That didn't get a smile from either of them, much less a laugh. 'This is Cliff Hardy, darling,' Mountain said. 'He's a private detective who does things like finding missing teenagers and throwing drunks out of rich people's parties.'

Kelly didn't seem to be listening; she played with her right nipple, poking and teasing at it until it stood out an inch from her breast. She moved rhythmically, as if she was listening to music being played inside her head.

'Do you know how dangerous this woman is?' I said. 'She's crazy, she has rape fantasies. She's the worst kind of trouble on legs.' I realised how silly it sounded as I said it, but I was desperately trying to touch bases, to stand up for normality in the bizarre surroundings. 'Come on, Bill, this isn't you. You're a writer, you need a keyboard and paper and something to drink.'

'I don't drink any more.' His voice was childlike with pleasure at forming the words. It was useless to try reaching him by referring to his earlier life. He pulled at the inelastic, slack skin on his face and twitched his tongue out of the corner of his mouth. A nerve jumped under his right eye: he was well away, responding to chemical and emotional stimuli all new and all his own.

Kelly knew how to get through to him; she massaged his upper arm with her long, strong fingers and carried his hand up to her breast. He gripped the nipple between thumb and forefinger and squeezed hard. I saw the pain wave hit her and give way to something else; a dreamy look came over her face and her purple tongue licked her lips as if they were sugar-coated. 'I want to hear all about it,' she said.

'All about what?' I said.

The tongue flicked out. 'How did he look, the man at the Blackheath house? The one Bill killed. How did he look?'

'He looked dead. And Bill'll look the same way if certain people catch up with him.'

Mountain grinned as if he'd caught me out in a lie. 'I thought you said you weren't working for them?'

'That's right. But I ran into a man named Grey who's working for the mob you've been playing games with. He doesn't want to play games; he thinks you know more about his operation than you should. He wants you dead.'

'So he sends you to do the job?' Kelly murmured.

'No, Jesus, It's too complicated a story to tell you now. Come on, this is ridiculous; you look very nice in your outfits but I'm freezing my arse off. Let's quit the play-acting and start thinking: I've got contacts, I can arrange a few things.'

Mountain wasn't listening. 'I had to imagine that part,' he said. 'The car thieves coming after me. Grey, you say? Good name, wish I'd thought of that. I wonder if I got it right otherwise?'

'I've seen your synopsis. You got it pretty right.'

'What about the people who supply the drugs to Dee and her crowd? They must be after me, I left clues.'

I shook my head, but I had to think of something to say instead of just sitting there like a trussed-up bale of wool. I sensed that his sympathies were with action and danger; passivity could be fatal. 'I don't know about them. God knows, Artie Henderson's not a very reliable associate. If they've got on to him somehow they could be getting close. Christ, Bill, how much trouble can you handle? And it's not just you, there's ....'

He gripped my jaw and ground the bones together. 'Yes, Hardy? There's who?'

Gripped like that I couldn't talk and it was no time to mention Erica anyway—Kelly would regard someone else's suffering as just part of the fun. Mountain went on grinding my face, but Kelly got impatient. He'd let go her nipple, and it looked as if she was jealous of the attention I was getting. She wandered away towards the whip rack; her bare buttocks above the tops of the shiny boots were a little flabby and there were bruises, precisely patterned, across them. Mountain gave my jaw a vicious twist and let go. He expected an answer.

'You're a sick man, Bill. I've seen Dr Holmes and he wants to talk to you. Maybe he can help. I'm sure he can help keep you out of gaol.' Mountain didn't react, and I only had the one card left to play. It was risky. I lowered my voice so Kelly couldn't hear. 'Erica wants to help too.'

My dry throat had brought the sound out in a harsh croak that carried more than I'd intended. Kelly came back in a few long strides. 'Why's he whispering?'

'He says Erica wants to help me.'

She laughed that cackling hoot again; it was a cruel, twisted sound full of pleasure at the thought of pain, and contempt for anything gentle. 'Erica,' she spat, 'if I had her here now I'd take her yellow hide off.'

'Yes,' Mountain said. 'You could. Where is she, Hardy?'

Looking up at the pair of them, I took a mental vow of silence. Nothing a rational person said could possibly make any kind of sense to them; they were travelling in a private dreamland signposted by drug fantasies and guided by obsessions that might have started in the womb. Kelly's fingers were sliding up and down a long, thin cane, and she was looking at Mountain with a rapt expression. He glanced at her and then down at his own body; the change that came over his face made me draw in breath sharply. He seemed to be filled with revulsion. He ran his hands over his chest and clawed at his nipples and the thick, grizzled hair. Kelly watched him, breathing hard.

'Have you slept with Erica, Hardy?'

I shook my head. 'You've got bigger problems, Mountain. You're headed for a padded cell, years of being treated like a child . . .'

'He has, he has!' Kelly almost shrieked. 'He's sucked her and she's . . .'

Mountain jerked the cane out of her hand; he acted decisively and then seemed to go dreamy again. It was eerie to watch his body following his mind in its wafting fluctuations. He flexed the cane and newly-tightened muscles moved under the old slack skin on his upper body. He looked down at me and spoke slowly, dreamily. 'I've finished the book.'

Kelly pouted. 'You didn't tell me.'

Mountain's face seemed to dissolve. 'I loaded up on speed and I blasted for thirty-six hours straight. I did the whole thing in thirty-six hours.'

'How does it end?' I said.

The face took on puzzlement briefly, then ecstasy. 'Don't know. Didn't read it when I finished. I want to celebrate.'

'Come on!' Kelly screamed. 'Come on!'

Mountain stepped forward and lifted the cane. I shrank away, pressing my back against the wall. Kelly swivelled around on one spiked heel and Mountain moved with her. They bent over, undulating like jazz dancers, and he slashed her savagely across the buttocks.

I was staring and I might have made some sort of noise. Mountain came out of his near-trance long enough to look at me. 'This is private,' he growled. I saw his arm swing back and then I could see the hairs on his hand, and then it felt as if one of those giant metal balls demolishers use had bounced off my skull.

25

T HE drug cut through the pain or the pain cut through the drug, I don't know which. I was in a state somewhere between consciousness and oblivion and slipping back and forwards between the two. I was closing my eyes a lot, because the things I thought I saw when I had them open were worse than the things I thought I saw when they were closed.

I heard a lot of yelling and opened my eyes. I saw two people moving around each other, hitting and screaming. I closed my eyes.

'You bastard!' she screamed as the whip hit her. She must have gathered saliva because I heard her spit it at him. He responded with a very hard slap.

'You shit!'

Swish.

'Turd! You shit-sucking turd!'

I kept my eyes closed. The shapes on the backs of my eyelids were definitely better, softer. But then my eyes stung and watered, and I had to look again. I'd seen people gripped by passions and lusts beyond their control before. In Malaya I'd seen men who were drunk on killing focus their whole being on the act. I'd seen opium smokers transfixed by the details of pipe preparation and tendrils of smoke in rooms that smelled of rat. I'd seen kleptomaniacs who trembled and wet themselves as they approached the objects they intended to steal, but who became coldly efficient at the critical moment. The passion of Kelly and Mountain was like that: an enclosed, excluding force field with its own laws and excruciating satisfactions.

The energy and excitement they generated and consumed threatened to spill over and seek some other outlet. It was distinctly uncomfortable being the only other outlet around. The drug was giving me the horrors, first of sight, now of sound. I couldn't stand the screaming and grunts. I crooned to myself dopily, and for a time everything became calm and quiet. I felt nothing; I was asleep somewhere soft and white.

Then I was awake again, and feeling pain everywhere. I had the power of movement back, although my vision was distorted and blurry. I struggled to get some give in the ropes, but there was none. I looked wildly around the room as their grunts and groans increased in tempo and loudness: the door was twenty feet off and shut tight; there was a whip on the floor a few feet away but, with me trussed up like that, it was about as useful as a Mars Bar.

Then I doubted that I was conscious, because I could see Mountain and Kelly in triplicate up on the bed. Six people on one bed. The Mountains were teasing the Kellys, moving up and down, advancing and withdrawing. The Kellys hammered with their free fists. The Mountains ignored the blows. They tensed and drove down. The Kellys screamed and flexed so hard the Mountains had to pin them with their whole bodies. Three free arms flopped over the side of the bed, and I could see the hands clenching and unclenching.

The images faded and I heard only sound, distantly, as if it was coming from another room—Kelly screamed and Mountain began to roar to blot out the sound. 'Finished,' he bellowed. 'Finished! Finished!' Then he yelled the word in French, and ranted away in what sounded like German, but could have been Russian or Polish for all I knew. His pounding rocked the bed and seemed to shake the floor. The room filled with the screams and roars and bumps. My vision came back, and in single image, but the action seemed suddenly to go into slow motion. I saw Kelly bend her arm and move it back to claw at the end of the mattress. She pulled out a knife with a long, broad blade and her knuckles cracked under the strain as she manipulated it in her palm. She got it right and jerked the arm and drove it down hard into Mountain's back; he bucked and the knife came free and she drove it down again. The muscles in Kelly's arm bunched and danced as she tugged the knife free and dug it in at a different angle and in a different place. Mountain arched up and yelled something that died in his throat. He flopped down on top of the woman and she dug and slashed at him.The blood spurted and flowed out of him; it puddled on the bed and dripped down onto the floor and flowed thickly across towards me.

Kelly sobbed and moaned and tried to get free of the corpse. She kicked and thrashed and it rolled clear of her. Her breath was coming in harsh gusts from her mouth and sibilant whistles from her nose. She hacked at the wrist rope, holding the knife the wrong way; the rope came free, but she cut herself in the process. Then she slashed through the ankle ropes, and cut herself some more. When she got to her knees on the bed, she was a nightmarish figure, streaked and smeared with blood from her head to her pubic hair. Her eyes stared wildly around the room. She pushed Mountain's body off the bed, and it fell with a thump.

I was struggling like a madman, almost dislocating my shoulders in the effort to get my hands under my feet and up in front me. Fear of the knife drove me; my only idea was to have some protection from it, even my tied hands. I got my hands clear; it felt as if I had crushed some vertebrae to do it and I'd certainly skinned my wrists up to the forearms. I pressed back and levered myself up to an almost standing position against the wall. She saw me and screamed. Maybe I screamed too. She launched herself from the bed, and came at me with the knife raised above her head. Her mouth was wide open, and her tongue protruded like a black snake.

She stumbled, re-gained balance and came on with the knife descending. I yelled this time for sure and pushed off the wall like a swimmer on the last turn; I lowered my head, went in under the knife, and butted her in the stomach driving as much of my weight into it as my trembling, cramped legs would permit. She staggered back and dropped the knife. I went to my knees but struggled up again. She was sagging, coming forward and I butted her again, and her own falling weight helped drive the wind and limb control out of her. She crumpled down to the carpet and lay still.

I scrambled across the floor, grabbed the knife and wriggled to the nearest corner like a hunted beast. I crouched there and panted, looking at the fallen woman and still feeling defenceless despite the knife. I gripped the handle with my feet and sawed through the wrist ropes, then I cut my feet free with a hacking chop that seared into my left ankle. Dee Kelly started to moan and move. I swapped the knife into my right hand; my vision was red-filmed with fear and pain and horror. She got to her knees and lumbered towards me as I pulled myself up. The blood-caked hair stood up on her head and her eyes bulged. I threw the knife away and did what Dempsey did to Firpo when he had him on his knees: I swivelled and put everything into a short left that landed flush on her blood-daubed jaw. Her head flicked back and she flopped to the floor and lay still.

26

When my heart rate had slowed to a hundred and my eyes were back in their sockets, I dragged myself over to look at Bill Mountain. His eyes were staring open and his jaw was locked in a dropping, askew position. In death, he looked depressed.

I rolled Deirdre Kelly's eyelids back and everything appeared to be normal under them. Her pulse was strong and her tongue was free in her mouth. A concussion at most. Her outstretched foot touched the whipping post, and I tied her ankle to it with a piece of bloodstained rope just to be sure.

Opening the door and walking out of that room was like hiking down a country trail on a mild Spring day. The passageway smelled of tobacco and marijuana smoke but there was no blood underfoot or on the walls. The party was long over and the apartment was a shambles, except for the bar, which had been tidied and cleaned. All the bottles and glasses had been washed, corked and stacked away. I wandered into the bathroom and found my clothes there, bundled up. I climbed into the space capsule shower and ran the water to scalding hot; I lathered and rinsed until all the blood was off me and I was clean and pink. The cuts on my wrists weren't bleeding but the one on my ankle was. I wadded up a paper napkin and put it over the cut under my sock.

It was way past the time I was supposed to call Grey, but I wasn't worried about it. I felt sure the trusty answering machine would be on the job and I had things to do first. I dressed and went to the bar for some whisky. I didn't notice the brand, but the scotch was the best I'd ever tasted. I had a short jolt, and then poured a long one and added some ice. I carried the drink with me, setting it down carefully and not marking surfaces as I searched the apartment. In the kitchen I found my gun; it was loaded and untampered with. I couldn't find the cassettes or Mountain's manuscript anywhere, and that left only one place to look.

As soon as I entered the black room I knew that something else had happened; there was a feeling of finality in the room such as a stage has at the end of a play when all the actors are out there taking their bows. Mountain lay exactly as I'd last seen him, but Kelly had stretched herself out at full length, leg, body and arm, and had reached the knife. Then she had rolled over onto her back; she probably hadn't even bothered to sit up. The knife lay by her outstetched hand and her throat was cut to the spinal cord.

I was glad I'd put on my shoes because the carpet was a sticky mess over most of its surface. I picked my way across the driest patches, and searched the bed. There was a concealed panel in the headboard, behind the fastenings for the ropes and chains. I worked on it with my pocket knife, and eventually splintered and prised it open. Inside was a big manila envelope containing a couple of hundred pages of typescript; a smaller package held two sound tapes and one video cassette.

I took the envelope and package back to the kitchen and sat down by the telephone. Then I remembered my drink which I'd left outside the black room. I fetched it, came back, and dialled the contact number. I got the recorded message and I told the machine that I had Mountain, and read off Deirdre Kelly's telephone number. Grey—and I was sure that it was Grey this time—called back immediately.

'Where are you?' he said.

'First things first. Let me talk to the girl.'

After a long pause Erica's voice came over the wire. 'I

was asleep,' she said.

'Lucky you. Are you all right?'

'Yes. What's going on? Have you found him?'

'Just do as you're told for a little while, and everything'll be all right. Put Grey back on, I'll see you soon.'

Grey came back on, and asked me where I was again. I finished my drink and laughed into the mouthpiece. 'Shut up and listen. You take the girl to this address.' I gave him Frank and Hilde's address in Harbord. 'You drop her there and go—drive away. You call me from the nearest phone you can find. If I've had a call from where you leave her and they tell me she's okay, I'll tell you where Mountain is.'

'Not good enough, Hardy. You're asking me to throw in my hand, and you might have nothing to show.'

'This has gone beyond tricks and games, Grey. Did you know Mountain had taken the Audi back? No? Well, he did. I've got plenty to show, don't worry. For example I've got a couple of tapes and a video cassette. You think I'd play funny buggers at this stage? I'm sick of this whole fucking business.'

'Mountain's there?'

'In person.'

'Subdued, I take it?'

'I'm almost past caring, Grey, take it or leave it.'

Something in my voice must have carried conviction. Grey agreed to my terms, and I cut him off and rang Frank Parker. Frank sounded sleepy and happy, the way a man might who was in the right bed with the right woman.

'Listen, Frank, I haven't got much time. Pretty soon a car'll pull up outside your joint, and a young woman'll knock at your door. She's Chinese, her name's Erica Fong. As soon as she's through the door ring this number. Got it?'

'Who's Chinese? What's going on?'

'No time. Have you got the bloody number?' I repeated it, and he sounded awake and unhappy, but he said he'd do it. I put the phone down and resisted the impulse to pour another drink. The adrenalin had started to run, and I was feeling pumped up and full of energy, which made the waiting I had to do hard. I checked the gun again and looked at the scotch bottle, again. I looked at it for quite a while, then the phone rang and I grabbed it.

'She's here, Cliff. She's okay. She wants to know about someone called Mountain. What . . . ?'

'Thanks, Frank. Get off the line!' I slammed the phone down and hovered my hand over it like someone playing Snap. But I let it ring a couple of times before I picked it up; when I answered my mouth was suddenly dry, and I could hardly form the words.

'She's delivered,' Grey said.

'Right. Here's the address.' I gave him the street and number. 'It's a block of flash flats. Park in the street and don't make a fuss.' He repeated the address and rang off quickly. I opened the front door and turned off the lights in the apartment except those in the hallway and the black room. The switches had dimmers and I dropped the hall down to a deep gloom and waited just inside the room opposite the black room. I had the tapes in my pocket and my S&W .38 in my hand.

When they came, it was the old reliable threesome of Grey, Peroni and Flabby. I heard a whispering out by the door and then soft footfalls on the hall carpet. They stood outside the black room; Peroni unshipped his gun and led the way in. Grey and Flabby followed and I heard them swear and bump into each other as they took in the sights. I went through the door with the gun ready and my heart rate up over the one hundred again.

'Surprise,' I said.

Peroni was the fastest, but not very fast; he turned around with his gun up at roughly the right elevation, but he saw that I had my gun pointing at his teeth before he could complete his move.

'Put the gun down, Peroni or you'll be just like them.'

He dropped the gun and it fell with a soggy plop to the blood-soaked floor. Flabby hardly noticed, he was too busy vomiting over by the whipping post.

'That helps,' I said. 'How d'you like it, Mr Grey?'

Grey's face was rigid with shock; he'd thrown his hands up to his face when he'd seen them, and the hands came down slowly now to hang uselessly at his sides.

'Did you ... ? Did ... ?'

'Uh huh. They did it all by themselves, just having a little harmless fun.'

'Jesus,' Peroni said. Flabby hung on the post and spat on the floor. Grey was struggling to recover his executive manner and finding it hard going. His adam's apple wobbled in his neck and he'd lost his old-young look. Now he just looked old. He controlled the movement in his neck by raising his hand and holding his throat.

'What do you want?' he said.

I reached into my pocket and took out the tapes. 'It's a question of what *you* want. Everything you asked for is here. There's Mountain and here's the tapes.' I tossed the tapes onto the bed; they hit with a splashy sound. 'Mountain's not going to be doing any talking and as far as I know he hasn't told anyone your secrets.'

'Secrets,' Grey said.

'Yeah. Now I've worked out a little bit about it—you've got bent cops and others to protect. I know that, and I couldn't care less.'

Grey gestured to Flabby to pick up the tapes, but Flabby shook his head. Grey walked over to the bed and picked them up. He was getting his nerve back fast. He looked down at Mountain whose face was in profile against the black carpet. He nodded slowly. Peroni shuffled his feet; his persecuted eyes were fixed on the body of Deirdre Kelly. He was excited by it.

'I think you should take Carl home,' I said. 'It ends here, Grey.'

Grey looked at me steadily. I could feel my control

going; my face was cold although the air in the room was warm and I was ready to start shaking inside. I didn't have much talk or authority left in me.

'The video,' Grey said.

'I've got it. You keep your bloody operation out of Sydney for six months and I'll mail it to you.'

'Mail?'

I had to hurry; I could feel myself unravelling. 'Right. Australia Post. I'll send it to Mr John Grey, General Delivery, Perth GPO. Okay?'

'Why Perth?'

'Perth'll do. You'll manage.'

'Yes,' Grey said. He took out a handkerchief and wiped the tapes. Then he put them in a pocket; he kept the bloodied handkerchief in his hand.

I gestured with the gun. 'On your way. This is the big city. I don't think you fit in.'

Flabby shuffled towards the door. Peroni tore his eyes away from Kelly, and looked at Grey who nodded. They moved after Flabby.

'I want my gun,' Peroni said.

'Tell you what I'll do, Carl. If you piss off now, I won't leave it here for the cops to find.'

They went down the hall and out of the apartment. I closed the door and listened for their steps on the gravel, and finally the sound of a car engine. A little fresh air had come in while the door was open, and I leaned against the wall and breathed it for a while with my eyes closed. Then I collected Peroni's gun, the video and Mountain's manuscript. I wiped the glass I'd used, doused the lights in the apartment and went out through the french windows at the side.

There was a promise of dawn in the sky, and the light night breeze already had a touch of warmth in it. There were a few lights burning in the apartments, but no sound

190

or movement. Ginny Ireland's silver VW was standing crookedly in its parking space and one mudguard was a crumpled ruin. There was a pair of shoes in the middle of the path to her door. I walked out to the street, and it took me a long time to get the key in the lock and open the door. My hand was shaking, so the ignition key jiggled automatically and the engine started sweetly.

I drove home watching for a tail and not seeing one, and so tired and shaken that I could hardly keep the car in top gear. I approached the house carefully, went in quickly with my two guns, and found the usual still emptiness. With the doors locked, I treated myself for shock and fatigue with aspirin and whisky, and slept for a couple of hours in my clothes on the couch. I woke up with the video cassette in my pocket digging into me and a shaft of light shining into my eyes.

The phone blipped briefly, but the machine picked up the call. I cleaned myself up, made coffee and sat down to look at Bill Mountain's book. It was typed on yellow A4 paper, double spaced and with wide margins. There was no title page and the pages were unnumbered. I leafed through it, page by page at first and then turning them over in ten page batches. The typescript had no chapter divisions and no headings. There was no punctuation. The lines of type switched from upper to lower case at random. It was written in English, French and German and at least half of it was in no language at all, gibberish.

THE BIG DROP
Peter Corris

A client happens to fall from the twentieth storey of a
building; a rock star goes missing; an erotic Mongol scroll
vanishes; a film star has a problem that has nothing to do
with creativity – it's all in a day's work for Cliff Hardy.
Yachts dance on the sparkling waters of the harbour, and
the back alleys are busy; the city's high and low classes go
about their daily business. But nothing really surprises
Hardy; and, for a hundred and twenty-five dollars a day (plus
expenses), he'll provide a few surprises of his own . . .

'Peter Corris is turning out some of the most entertaining
fiction in Australia today . . .'
The Age

Published by Unwin Paperbacks.

THE EMPTY BEACH
Peter Corris

It began as a routine investigation into supposed drowning.
But Cliff Hardy, private detective, soon found himself
literally fighting for his life in the murky, violent underworld
of Bondi.
The truth about John Singer, black marketeer and poker
machine king, is out there somewhere – amidst the drug
addicts and prostitutes and alcoholics. Hardy's job is to stay
alive long enough in the world of easy death to get to
the truth.
The truth hurts . . .

'. . . a fine, tightly-controlled story.'
West Australian

MAKE ME RICH
Peter Corris

Cliff Hardy is at the party to look after the paintings and
throw out the drunks – gently.
But there he meets Helen Broadway, who interests him; and
Paul Guthrie, who wants Hardy to look for his step-son, Ray.
Hardy delves into the sleazy world of Kings Cross
backstreets and lowdown pubs, following a twisting path
laid by a hitman, a criminal with heavy political protection,
and a seedy alcoholic member of his own profession.
There's scarcely enough time for Helen Broadway,
interesting though she still is.
Hardy pushes on to the final confrontation. It's rough: the
guns are out, and the odds are no help . . .

'. . . there is nothing random or haphazard about the way
Corris tells his story; it is a piece of masterly, disciplined and
highly effective narrative.'
The Australian

Published by Unwin Paperbacks.

HEROIN ANNIE
Peter Corris

Cliff Hardy in action again: trying to keep one step ahead of his client's troubles – and his own.
He has to cope with the brute force exercised in sleazy back streets to the more refined form of violence to be found in the boardroom of city skyscrapers. Along the way he has to deal with everyone from fashion models and teenaged junkies to urban developers and crooked funeral directors. Some are friendly and helpful, some try to kill him . . .
Hardy copes, with his guts and his savvy, and all for a hundred and twenty five dollars a day (plus expenses) . . .

Published by Unwin Paperbacks.

THE WINNING SIDE
Peter Corris

The Winning Side is a moving and compassionate account
of a man caught between two worlds.
Charlie Thomas, born in a humpy camp to Aboriginal
parents in the 1920's, learns to fight early. He fights in the
backblocks of Queensland during the Depression, and in
the Middle East and Pacific in World War Two.
As a decorated veteran, he fights on in the cities and the
country against racial prejudice, authority and his own
weaknesses. He has to fight; white Australia tries to keep
him on the losing side – in the boxing tents, pubs and gaols.
Charlie Thomas fights for education, justice, hope and love
– to make his side the winning side.

Published by Unwin Paperbacks.

ROOM TO MOVE

Women's Short Stories

These thirty-two short stories have been selected by Suzanne Falkiner to present a balanced collection of modern writing by *Australian* women. They include a selection of some of Australia's best known names (Jolley, Astley, Zwicky) through to the most promising emerging writers (Garner, Sperling, Viidikas, Grenville) and some of the more avant garde and experimental of the new voices (Inez Baranay, Jeri Kroll, Finola Moorhead). A proportion, including those of Garner and Zwicky, have never been published before. Most have had previous publication in small magazines, and have been selected by their authors as among those they most wish to perpetuate.

Published by Unwin Paperbacks.

FLESH IN ARMOUR

Flesh in Armour is the graphic and compelling story of what it was like to be a soldier in the bloodbath of World War One. The vast and chaotic landscape of the Western Front is seen through the eyes of three Australian soldiers: Frank Jeffreys, sensitive and unable to bear the strains of war; Charl Bently, untroubled by the complexities that surround them all; and Jim Blount, who finds his true self – and dies in action. It is a novel of heroic deeds – and the sheer struggle for survival in the senseless carnage of Europe at War. Leanard Mann fought in the mud and destruction of Flanders, and this unerringly accurate novel bears the unmistakable ring of truth.

Published by Unwin Paperbacks.

SHALLOWS

Tim Winton

On the south coast of Western Australia a battle has begun. Conservationists and whalers confront each other on the seas, townspeople bicker and connive in the streets, while in the midst of it all, a marriage collapses and an old man, stalked by death, flees his past and the God of his forefathers.

This complex and ambitious novel won Tim Winton the 1984 Miles Franklin Award, confirming him as one of Australia's most promising literary talents.

'Shallows is a profound and inspiring work of fiction.'
David Myers, *The Age*
'I finished this book with a rare sense of elation.'
Donna Sadka, *West Australian*
'. . . his fiction is full of care, in all three senses – of craftsmanship, of moral concern, and of a sobriety before the facts of life.'
Don Anderson, *National Times*

BIRDS OF PASSAGE

Brian Castro

Birds of Passage is the powerful and haunting story of
Seamus O'Young, an Australian-born Chinese, on a
collision course with the past.
He reconstructs his past through the eyes of Shan, an
ancestor who came to Australia in the 1850's. And, just as
Shan was driven from the goldfields by depravity, racism
and sheer greed; so Seamus finds himself, a century later,
fighting for his own life and sanity.
Birds of Passage was a joint winner of the 1982 Australian/
Vogel Literary Award.

AL JAZZAR

Suddenly, the Middle East is teetering on the brink of all-out war – and this time, it may be too late to pull back . . .

- The leadership of the PLO has been swept aside by one of the new breed of guerilla fighters – the sophisticated and ruthless AL JAZZAR (The Butcher).
- Simultaneous PLO attacks in Jordan and France unleash a bitter struggle to overthrow the Hashemite monarchy, and raise the spectre of uncontrolled terrorism raging through European capitals.
- A Russian spy is exposed at the heart of the Israeli government – shaking the Jewish state to its very foundations.

In the midst of all this, Israel is threatened with a desperate, bloody battle for survival against forces which seek the complete liberation of all Palestine . . .

As AL JAZZAR surges towards its savage, unexpected conclusion, this alarmingly believable novel shows that in the volatile world of Middle East politics, nothing can be taken for granted . . .

AL JAZZAR was joint winner of the Australian/Vogel Award for 1981.

Published by Unwin Paperbacks.

MATILDA, MY DARLING
Nigel Krauth

Matilda, My Darling is a stirring and imaginative story, set amid the turmoil and tension of the shearers' strike of the 1890's.

Private detective Hammond Niall begins what he thinks is a routine investigation into a bush murder. But he and his travelling companion, 'Banjo' Paterson, are soon caught up in a world which seems to be sliding into civil war.

As the plot unfolds against this background of violence and confrontation the murder investigation becomes an enquiry into the very basis of the society of the day. And for Paterson, the period means both the trauma of the end of his engagement – and the writing of 'Waltzing Matilda'.

Matilda, My Darling was a joint winner of the 1982 Australian/Vogel Literary Award.